Based on the characters
by Robert Rodriguez

Written by Elizabeth Lenhard

HYPERION
MIRAMAX BOOKS
New York

For information address Hyperion Paperbacks for Children,
114 Fifth Avenue, New York, New York 10011-5690.

Printed in the United States of America

First Edition

1 3 5 7 9 10 8 6 4 2

This book is set in 13/17 New Baskerville.

ISBN 0-7868-1717-8

Visit www.spykids.com

Juni Cortez, boy spy, wiped a bead of sweat off his brow. He glanced, for the third time, at the manual propped in front of him. Then he turned to a small computer at his elbow and typed in some instructions.

A robotic arm jutting out of the wall of Juni's work area swung over and delicately poured a precise amount of bright red powder into his concoction. Juni picked up a metal instrument and began to stir the formula carefully.

All it would take, he thought nervously, is one wrong measurement or one false move and all would be lost!

Juni's concentration on the task at hand was so intense, he barely heard his sister, Carmen, enter the room. She peered over his shoulder and said, "Is it ready yet?"

"*Aigh!*" Juni cried. He jumped away from the counter and spun to face his sister. He was holding a bottle of greenish gold liquid in one hand, a measuring cup in the other.

"You could have made me spill this!" Juni said. "Do you know how rare this solution is?"

Carmen rolled her almond-shaped brown eyes.

"Juni," she said dryly, "that's olive oil."

"*Imported* olive oil," Juni retorted. "Mom had this stuff shipped in from an obscure Greek island! It sat in Customs for six months!"

"Still," Carmen said, "it's not like you were disengaging a thermogigawatt reactor that could throw the earth into the next Ice Age!"

"True," Juni said, turning back to his work. "I did that last month. But in some ways, this is an even bigger challenge—paella! The most delicious, hard-to-cook dish in all of Spanish cuisine."

Carmen snorted and looked down at her younger brother. He wasn't wearing their usual uniform—black cargo pants, long-sleeved T-shirt, and a gadget-laden spy vest. Instead, he was clomping around in clogs, black-and-white-checked chef's pants, and a white smock. From the loops of his utility belt—where Juni usually kept a periscope, laser beam cutter, personal robot remote control, and other gadgets—hung a whisk, a lemon zester, and a sheathed chef's knife. And atop his sproingy, red curls was a tall, white, cylindrical toque.

"Juni, you're obsessed with cooking!" Carmen said. She wandered to the end of the kitchen counter where Juni was working. Then she gazed around the room. Secretly, she didn't blame Juni for spending all his time in the kitchen lately. The room, filled with colorful Spanish tiles, Mexican pottery, and oversized, comfy kitchen chairs, was the central hub of their dramatic cliff-top mansion. It was cozy and grand at the same time. The whole family liked to hang out there.

The kitchen was even outfitted with a computer, cleverly disguised as a microwave oven. And the computer was a direct connection to the OSS—the top-secret government agency where the kids and their parents worked as spies. From this computer, the Spy Kids had been sent on missions to save the world from crazed TV stars, power-hungry double agents, evil veterinarians, and other sinister types.

But lately, the only thing coming out of their microwave/computer had been buttered popcorn.

The Spy Kids were missionless.

"I wish we had something to do," Carmen said, slumping back against the counter. "We haven't saved the world in weeks."

"Don't be so melodramatic," Juni said, waving a wooden spoon at her. "So, business happens to be a little slow. But it could be worse. After all, Mom and Dad went ten *years* without a mission."

Juni was right. Once upon a time, Ingrid and Gregorio Cortez had been the most skillful spies the world had ever seen. But then they'd met each other. They'd fallen in love and gotten married. And when Carmen and Juni were born, they'd decided to get out of the spy business altogether. They'd settled down to a nice, safe life of parent-teacher conferences, family picnics, and working from home as consultants.

But a couple years ago, a mission had come along that Mom and Dad just couldn't resist. They'd left the kids home to go save the world. But when the mission went sour, Carmen and Juni had become spies themselves. And they had saved their parents.

Now the four Cortezes worked together as a spy team.

That is, *when* there was spy work to be done.

Carmen gazed hopefully at the red lights and sirens stationed by each doorway. In the event of an emergency, the OSS contacted them by flashing the lights and blaring the sirens. But now, all she could hear was the sizzle of chorizo sausage in Juni's paella.

"I wish we could have just one red alert," she whined. "Just a *little* one."

"I don't," Juni said, spritzing his skillet with fresh lime juice and whisking off his toque. "Not now, at least. It's suppertime!"

Juni pressed a button on the elaborate spy watch that was always strapped to his wrist.

"Mom, Dad?" he said into the watch's tiny speaker.

A deep voice with a Spanish accent rumbled out of the watch.

"Yes, Juni," Dad said. "Your mother and I are doing some computer hacking to keep ourselves limber during the dry spell."

"Well, I hope you've worked up an appetite," Juni replied. "Please report to the dining room, immediately. Over."

While Juni sifted through the kitchen drawers for serving spoons, Carmen headed into the dining room. She gasped.

"Juni really does have too much time on his hands," she muttered. Her brother had set the table for a feast. Half a dozen candles burned in a silver candelabra. Mom and Dad's best French crystal and

Mexican dishes were arranged before each chair. On top of each plate was a linen napkin folded to resemble a swan or water lily. A bottle of sparkling apple juice was chilling in an ice bucket.

As Carmen sat down at her place, her parents joined her with bemused looks on their faces.

Then Chef Juni entered the room. He carried a large tray topped by a dome-shaped, silver cover. He stalked over to the head of the table and placed the tray before his father.

"Dad," he said seriously.

"Junito," Dad replied.

"I give you my soon-to-be-famous—paella!" Juni cried. He whisked the cover off the tray to reveal a mouthwatering mixture of golden rice, sizzly sausage, plump shrimp, still-steaming clams and mussels, and a sprinkling of red peppers and onions.

Juni puffed out his chest with pride.

Mom gasped and began to applaud.

Even Carmen had to admit the paella smelled fabulous.

But Dad said nothing. He merely stared at the tray of succulent, Spanish supper in silence.

And then—he burst into tears!

"Dad . . ." Juni gulped. He stared at his father's heaving shoulders. Then he looked at his tray of paella. His heart sank. Before he'd even tasted it, his father had decided Juni's cooking stank!

Juni cast his eyes downward and whispered, "I'm sorry."

Dad shook his head and blew his nose with his napkin. He reached out and squeezed his son's hand.

"Don't apologize, Juni," he said with a sniffle. "Your dinner—it smells exactly like the paella my mother makes back in Madrid. Ah, I can almost taste it!"

"You *can* taste it, honey," Mom said, scooping some of the scented rice and seafood onto Dad's plate. Dad grabbed his fork and took a bite. Then he burst into tears again!

"Delicious!" he wept.

Mom patted Dad's shoulder and winked at the kids.

"You know how your dad gets," she said.

"Very emotional," Carmen and Juni said at once. They glanced at each other and tried not to giggle.

Finally, Dad wiped his eyes and smiled at his family. Then everyone dug into the paella.

"You know what would be great, Dad?" Carmen said. "If we went to visit Nana."

"In Madrid?" Mom said, raising one of her perfectly arched, auburn eyebrows. "Carmen, that's quite a trip!"

"Yeah, and it's the perfect time to take it!" Juni said before stuffing a sausage into his mouth. "After all, the spy business has been pretty slow lately."

"You both have a point," Mom said. Then she turned to her husband. "You know, Gregorio, your mother hasn't seen the kids in a couple of years. They've grown so much!"

"And *we* haven't had a vacation in a couple of years," Dad said, gazing at his wife over the rim of his glass of sparkling apple juice. "It would be romantic!"

"Uh, hello?" Carmen said. "We're eating! Could we save the mushy stuff until after we digest?"

"Sorry," Mom said, clearing her throat and fluffing her red curls absentmindedly. "I think what your father is saying is—we're going to Spain!"

"Cool!" Juni cried. "Wait till we tell Nana about all our adventures," he added giddily. "She'll flip! I mean, the last time we saw her, Carmen and I weren't spies. We were just ordinary schoolkids."

Juni watched his father's expression change. In a trembly voice, Juni said, "Uh, is there a problem, Dad?"

"There will be," Dad replied in a low voice, "if you tell your Nana about your adventures." He leaned forward, pausing to look into Carmen and Juni's eyes. "We must keep our identities a secret from your Nana. You can never tell her that we are spies. *Never!*"

CHAPTER 2

A few days later, the Cortez family was walking through the Madrid airport.

"Ugh," Carmen said. Her feet dragged as the family made their way to Customs. "I haven't been this jet-lagged since we went on that mission to the Australian bush!"

"Oh, pshaw," Mom said as she handed her passport to a Customs officer. "The minute you get out into the streets of Madrid, you'll forget how tired you are. It's a city of *mucho* fun and *mucho* madness!"

"Madrid is also where we fell in love," Dad said, giving Mom a gushy look. "Remember, darling? We were at that little café? I was sitting by the exit, and you were next to the kitchen. You were disguised as a Russian countess."

"And you," Mom said coyly, "a mariachi."

"Huh?" Juni blurted. He was rubbing his tired eyes.

"Don't you remember our old bedtime story?" Carmen said to her brother. "Mom and Dad had to date each other in secret because their countries were at odds."

"Oh, yeah," Juni said. Then he turned to his parents. "Hey! I thought we agreed. No mushy stuff on our vacation!"

"Oh, all right," Mom said, rolling her eyes.

"I don't think they know I mean it," Juni whispered to his sister. By now, they had passed through Customs and were just arriving at the baggage-claim carousel.

"Good luck!" Carmen said. Just then, she saw a sleek, black duffel bag coming toward them on the carousel's conveyer belt. "Ooh, there's my bag! Grab it!"

But before Juni could snag his sister's suitcase, another hand reached for it. The hand belonged to a tall, wiry man with eyes that were such a bright amber color, they looked orange. His glasses were tinted blue and his fingernails were painted green. But the strangest thing about him was his chin, which was so long and pointed, it practically hit his chest.

Carmen gasped in alarm. But quickly, her spy spirit kicked in. She walked up to the strange-looking man and said in Spanish, "You chose the wrong bag to filch."

"Oh," the thief replied, "I'm not stealing. I'm just getting your attention."

"Well, you got it," Carmen growled, dropping into a kung fu fighting stance. "But trust me, *señor*. In about thirty seconds, you're gonna wish you didn't!"

"Easy, *niña*," the strange man said slyly. "Tell you what. I'll play you a song and we'll call it even."

In one motion, the stranger tossed Carmen her bag and whipped a long, golden flute out of the breast pocket of his tattered jacket. Then he pursed his thin, pale lips and began to play a lilting Spanish dance.

"Oh," Carmen said, feeling a bit confused. "I thought . . ."

Suddenly, Dad stalked over.

"All right, all right," he said. He flipped a few coins at the musician. "*Gracias,*" Dad said, "and move it along now, please."

Curling his lip at Dad, the man shuffled out of the baggage claim area.

"What a creep," Juni said.

"You can say that again," Carmen said.

"What a creep," Juni stated, obeying orders.

Carmen smacked her brother on the arm. "Little brothers," she mumbled.

Dad looked down at the Spy Kids with a serious expression.

"Children," he said, "Madrid is crawling with pickpockets and scoundrels. A lot of them pose as artists or buskers—you know, street musicians. They're no good. Even if you *are* spies, you should still be careful of them."

As Carmen and Juni nodded somberly, Mom walked over. She was wheeling a duffel bag–laden luggage cart.

"We've got all our things," she said. "Let's grab a cab and head to Nana's."

From the backseat of a tiny, but very speedy, European taxi, Carmen and Juni gaped at the sights of Madrid flying by.

"It's been so long since we've been here," Juni said, "I barely remember it. What's that building over there?"

He pointed at an ornate cathedral with a gigantic dome.

"Ah, that's the biggest church in the city, the Basílica de San Francisco el Grande," Dad said.

"There are a couple masterpieces by my favorite Spanish painter in there—Goya."

A few minutes later, Carmen pointed out the window.

"I remember that," she said, gazing at a looming museum. "The Prado, right, Dad?"

"Ah, *sí*," Dad said. "Oh, and look, children, there's the Parque del Buen Retiro. The biggest park in Madrid. My friends and I used to go there after school every day. We'd hang out, eat Cheerios, and play soccer."

Dad's face softened as memories washed over him. His eyes grew moist and sparkly.

"Oh, boy," Juni said, eyeing his dad's trembling lower lip. "Here we go. It's the paella all over again."

But before Dad could burst into tears, the taxi turned a corner. And Dad was struck by another building that came into view before them.

Most of the architecture in old Madrid was grand and ancient—great, stone facades decorated with scrolls and cupolas. Or quaint European buildings fronted by small, shuttered windows and laundry-festooned clotheslines.

But this building was entirely different.

It looked like a tiered wedding cake. Decorating

each layer were wobbly polka dots, curlicues, or abstract gargoyles.

The layers were also splashed with colors—the pinks and oranges and greens of psychedelic sherbet or mischief-spiked Play-Doh.

"It's a new E. Goísta!" Dad breathed. "It's . . . magnificent!"

"It's . . . bizarre!" Juni said. "What's an E. Goísta, Dad?"

"Not what," Carmen said. "Who! E. Goísta is a famous architect. Don't you remember seeing his crazy buildings the last time we were in Madrid?"

Juni shrugged as Dad stared at the building in awe.

"E. Goísta was just starting to build his amazing structures when I left Madrid to go into the spy business," Dad said. "Now, his work is all over the city. He's really changed the landscape of the entire city."

Juni looked from a pretty nineteenth-century apartment building—bedecked with scrolly iron balconies and fluffy potted flowers—to E. Goísta's garish glop of a building.

"Huh," he said with a frown. "I don't see the appeal. Maybe I'm too hungry to appreciate art."

"I'm *sure* your Nana will have a snack ready for

you when we get to her apartment," Mom said with a grin.

"Maybe a *bocadillo de jamón*," Juni said dreamily, "or some *tortilla de patatas*."

"Show-off," Carmen muttered. "That's just a fancy way of saying ham sandwich and potato omelet."

"We *are* in Spain," Juni retorted. "And we *are* spies. As in multilingual and totally worldly."

"Ah-ah-ah," Dad cautioned. He wagged a finger at his children. "Remember, the spy part must remain a secret. You cannot breathe a word to your grandmother."

Carmen and Juni exchanged a look. They'd been so shocked by Dad's order at dinner a few nights ago, they hadn't questioned it at the time. But now, Carmen couldn't resist cautiously asking, "Can you tell us why, Dad?"

Dad fell silent for a moment. As the taxi continued to hurtle through the bustling Madrid streets, he glanced broodingly out the window at a string of shop fronts.

"You see that store?" he suddenly asked. He pointed at one nondescript window. "My father worked there."

"Really?" Carmen and Juni said together.

They peered through the cab window. Hanging in the shop window were strings of plump sausages, big pink hams, and a few plucked chickens.

"Your father was a butcher?" Carmen said to Dad. "I didn't know that!"

The Spy Kids' grandfather had died before they were born. Over the years, Dad had told them many stories about their Grandpapi. But none had involved a butcher shop.

"A butcher . . ." Dad said sadly. "That's what he told us, yes. Every day, he put on his white apron and grabbed his lunch pail and went off to the butcher shop. But one day, one terrible day when I was about eight years old, he forgot his pail. My mother gave me the address of Papi's shop and sent me to bring him his lunch."

"And . . . ?" Juni said.

"And when I arrived, nobody was at the butcher counter," Dad said. "So I wandered into the back room. Being small, I noticed a trapdoor beneath a worktable. I peeked into it. I saw nothing but blackness. It was some sort of tunnel. And before I knew it, I had fallen in! It turned out to be a hydraulic chute leading to a massive, underground office complex."

"Oh!" Carmen exclaimed.

Mom nodded and said quietly, "The butcher shop was just a front for the secret offices of *OSS España*."

"The Spanish OSS!" Juni breathed. "Which means our grandpa . . ."

"Was a spy!" Dad said.

CHAPTER 3

"I never knew our spy genes went back further than you and Mom!" Carmen said. She gazed at her dad across the taxi's backseat.

"Yes," Dad said with a brusque nod. "When I landed in the OSS's secret offices, I began to, well, *spy*. That's how I learned that my Papi was a hero. He had saved the world many times over. I was so proud, I ran home and told my mother everything I had seen."

"And she was . . . happy?" Juni asked his father gently.

"Perhaps she would have been," Dad said with a grimace, "if she hadn't been worried sick! She never had a moment's peace after she knew Papi was a spy. After all, my father skirted danger and cheated death on a daily basis! My mother, meanwhile, paced back and forth and wrung her hands constantly. She was *so* emotional. She would burst into tears at a moment's notice."

"So that's genetic, too!" Juni whispered to Carmen with a grin.

"I felt so guilty for worrying my mother," Dad continued. "When I became a spy, I vowed to do everything in my power to keep the truth from her."

"And," Mom began, "you can understand that if she knew her *grandchildren* were spies—"

"It would cause her terrible grief!" Dad groaned. "So, please, children, I beg you, for the sake of your Nana, no spy talk while we are in Spain. That shouldn't be too hard. We are on vacation, after all!"

Screeeeech!

The taxi suddenly lurched to a halt, sending Dad careening into the glass panel that separated the front seat from the back. His face smushed against the glass cartoonishly. And Dad sighed, "Ah, how I love Madrid."

Carmen glanced at Juni and rolled her eyes. Grown-ups were so weird.

Before Juni could mutter a comment, the taxi's back door popped open.

"*Mi familia!*" screeched a sweet, happy voice. Before the Spy Kids knew what was happening, they'd been swept out of the cab and into the soft, squishy embrace of their beloved Nana.

As tall and muscly as their Dad was, that's how short and soft their grandmother was. She was built like a big, sumptuous feather pillow. She wore her silver hair in a long braid down her back and dressed in flowing, breezy, bright-colored dresses. She smelled like chilies and chocolate. She was everything a grandma ought to be.

Especially since the first words out of her mouth were, "You must be so hungry. Come in, come in— I feed you!"

"Whoo-hoo!" Juni said. But when Nana released him to go kiss Dad on both cheeks and coo over Mom, Carmen grabbed Juni's elbow and pulled him to the edge of the sidewalk.

"I'm worried about all this," she whispered into her brother's ear. "We never take our spy watches off. I'm a hacker, and you're a kung fu master. Spying's in our blood. It's who we are. How can we hide all that from Nana?"

"Please," Juni said as he trotted down the terra-cotta-tiled walkway toward Nana's cozy little apartment building. "Nana's seventy years old and as sweet as caramel custard. She won't suspect a thing. It'll be a piece of cake—"

BEEEP, BEEEP, BEEEEEP, BEEEEEEEP!

The four spies froze.

That was the sound of their OSS pagers, stashed in their purses, packs, and pockets.

And the shrill beeping wasn't just that of any page. It was a red alert! Something, or someone, was in big trouble, and the Cortezes were needed.

"What is that?" Nana cried, slapping her plump hands over her ears.

"It's . . . a car alarm!" Carmen shrieked.

"It's . . . a fire a block away," Juni cried.

Mom merely turned bright red and slapped her hip pocket frantically. Somehow, she hit the button that turned her pager off.

But the other three were still blaring away.

So Dad stepped in.

"Let me handle this," he muttered to his wife and kids. Then he pasted on a falsely reassuring smile and turned toward Nana.

"Uh, Mama," he said, putting his arm around Nana's shoulders and steering her toward the apartment building. "You know how I am a computer consultant?"

"*Sí, sí,*" Nana said, reaching up to pinch Dad's cheek. "My smart American son!"

"Heh, heh," Dad said, as a red welt appeared on

his cheek. He glanced shiftily at his family and continued.

"Well, you know me, always puttering. So I set our watches with alarms . . . jet-lag alarms!" he said. "That way, we, uh, would know when to take a nap. Which is . . . exactly what we have to do right now!"

"Yes," Mom piped up. "Just a quick catnap before we sit down to dinner, Mama. We remember where our rooms are. You won't mind leaving us undisturbed?"

"Not at all," Nana said. "It'll give me more time to whip up something special for my Gregorio to have for dinner!"

Dad smiled sweetly at his mother. But when he turned to his family, his face was ashen.

"This," he said in a trembling whisper, "is going to be *no* piece of cake."

As soon as they made sure that Nana was occupied in the kitchen, the Cortezes rushed to Mom and Dad's bedroom, which was actually Dad's childhood bedroom. The room was still outfitted with twin bunk beds and plastered with yellowed soccer posters. One shelf groaned beneath some dusty, old trophies.

"Dad!" Carmen cried, picking up a gold trophy with a tiny matador on top. "I didn't know you were a champion bullfighter!"

"Or an award-winning junior chemist!" Juni said. He picked up a tarnished silver test tube and polished it with his shirt cuff.

"Or . . . a really bad dresser!" Mom said. Her husband and kids spun around to find Mom staring with a curled lip into one of the suitcases she'd just opened. Resting on top of some clothes and a shaving kit was a truly horrible hat. It was red, white, and blue. It had earflaps and a big, floppy brim. And to top it all off, the brim had a little electric fan clipped to it.

"Dad!" Carmen gasped. "Are you really going to wear that in Madrid, one of the most cosmopolitan cities in Europe? Everyone will think we're tacky tourists!"

"Of course, I'm going to wear it," Dad said. He swiped the awful hat out of the suitcase and planted it over his wavy, black hair. Then he winked at his family and tugged gently on one of the earflaps. A gentle humming sound filled the room. Then, a tiny satellite dish popped out of the hat right above the flap!

A tug on the other earflap revealed a little television screen ready to receive satellite images.

Next, Dad tapped his fingers underneath the hat's brim—it was a computer keyboard! The family heard the familiar beeps and whirs of a wireless modem dialing up.

"Hot off the presses from your Uncle Machete," Dad explained. "This is a complete international-spy communications center, cleverly disguised as a tacky tourist's hat." Uncle Machete was Dad's older brother. He was also a brilliant gadget inventor. True, sometimes Uncle Machete's gizmos were highly flawed. But this ugly hat seemed to be working like a charm."

"Cool!" Juni breathed. He pointed at the hat's goofy brim. "What does that little fan do?"

"It keeps me cool while I am doing spy work," Dad said. He flicked the fan on and smiled as a jet of air shot into his face, ruffling his eyebrows wildly. Carmen was just about to collapse into major giggles when the chiseled face of Devlin—the Cortezes' boss at the OSS—suddenly appeared on the tiny TV screen.

"Cortezes!" Devlin said. He looked grave. "Thank goodness, I was able to reach you. I see from my spy tracker that you landed in Spain an hour ago."

"Yes, Devlin," Mom said. "We just arrived. What's happened?"

"Nothing, yet," Devlin said. "But disaster is looming over Madrid. If you can't stop it, the entire city is doomed!"

CHAPTER 4

"**A**ll of Madrid, doomed?" Dad squeaked after Devlin delivered his sinister news. "My mother and cousins? My childhood friends? My homeland?!? It cannot be."

"It *will* not be!" Juni declared. He gazed determinedly at his father's stricken face. Then he gritted his teeth and turned to the tiny screen jutting out of Dad's hat.

"Mr. Devlin, sir!" he said. "We're ready for our mission. What's threatening Madrid?"

"Okay, spies, hang on to your hats," Devlin said. "Especially you, Gregorio. There's a supervillain in town, and his name is E. Goísta!"

"The architect?!" blurted the entire Cortez family.

"The *mad* architect," Devlin corrected them. "As you probably know, E. Goísta has created an empire in Madrid. His fantastic buildings span the city. They are regarded as great works of contemporary art, and E. Goísta as one of the world's supreme craftsmen."

"What could possibly be wrong with that?" Carmen asked.

"Our intelligence has just determined that E. Goísta's buildings are more than just buildings," Devlin explained. "They are instruments of evil! They are made, not of concrete or bricks or stucco, but of a high-tech, porous substance. And that substance has been infused with powerful chemicals. When activated, every E. Goísta building in Madrid will release this stuff into the air. The city will be covered by a highly noxious cloud of green, smelly gas."

"What will these chemicals do?" Juni asked.

"They'll put every man, woman, child, and animal in the city limits to sleep," Devlin responded. "Permanently!"

Dad gasped.

Mom gulped.

Juni flopped onto the bunk bed.

And Carmen blurted, "Talk about a siesta!"

"Actually, there's no time to talk about it," Devlin said brusquely. "We've reason to believe that E. Goísta is ready to enact his fiendish plan any day now. He's just announced his retirement.

Which means he's built all the buildings he wants to build.

"In other words," he continued, gritting his teeth, "the first part of his plan is complete. Now it's time for the maniacal artist's next—and final—step."

Devlin turned to his computer and began typing briskly. In a few seconds, another gentle whirring sound filled the bedroom. A large piece of paper began scrolling out of the back of Dad's tacky tourist hat.

"I've just wired you a topographical map of Madrid," Devlin said as Juni pulled the sheet out of Dad's hat. "The location of each E. Goísta building is highlighted in yellow."

Juni scrutinized the map, then looked up at the screen.

"I'm assuming we can find E. Goísta himself in one of these buildings?" Juni asked.

"Uh, we hope," Devlin said. "The truth is, E. Goísta's location is unknown."

"Nobody knows where he lives?" Carmen gasped.

"Nobody," Devlin answered. "He's a notorious hermit. He's never been photographed. The only thing we *do* know is he's a huge gourmet. He's got a weakness for fabulous food."

"And that's our only intel?" Mom asked.

"That's it," Devlin admitted. "The rest is up to you."

Then, with a sharp electronic sputter, the tiny TV screen went black.

"Over and out," Carmen said broodingly. Her shoulders slumped in disappointment.

"Yeah, and so much for our vacation," Juni said. "It's time to save the world again. Or, at least, Madrid."

"And there's no time to lose," Mom said. She was already striding across the room to her suitcase. She flipped it open and pulled out her utility belt. She began loading it with laser lassos, gripper-climbers, suction-cup darts, and other sophisticated spy gadgets. "If we're going to find E. Goísta, we need to act immediately."

Suddenly, the bedroom door slammed open.

"Gregorio!"

"Mama!" Dad yelled. He spun around to face his mother, who was standing in the doorway, carrying a sizzling cast-iron skillet. Quickly, he yanked on the earflaps of his hat, retracting the satellite dish and TV screen.

At the same time, Mom whipped her utility belt under the bunk bed. Then she threw her arms into the air and began stretching with exaggerated luxury.

"Mmmm, great nap," she said.

"Yes, in fact, I think we're ready to do a little sight-seeing," Dad piped up.

"You can tell by the tacky tourist hat," Juni cried. He pointed at his dad's floppy head helpfully.

Nana's face fell.

"Ooh, you're running out already?" she said. "But I made your favorite. Paella!"

Nana held out the skillet of saffron rice, seafood, and sausage. Its aroma wafted through the room. Dad's face slackened. His eyes went moist. And he turned to his family.

"Yes, you are partly right, Ingrid," he said. "We have to act . . . right after dinner."

A couple of hours later, the spies were thoroughly stuffed. Nana had served them gazpacho, paella, fish baked in salt, melon wrapped in ham, and countless other Spanish delicacies. Now she was presenting them with cups of creamy caramel flan. Juni took a big bite of the baked custard, then closed his eyes in delight.

"Nana," he said, "this is the best flan I ever ate. You'll *have* to give me the recipe."

Nana patted Juni on the head. Then she shook her finger at the rest of the family.

"Eat, eat!" she urged them as they picked at their desserts. "You are all too skinny. Now, tell me, what would you like to do while you're in Madrid?"

"Well . . ." Mom said, giving Dad a sidelong glance.

"Juni and I wanted to check out some of the E. Goísta buildings!" Carmen piped up.

"Excellent!" Nana said. "You could start right down the street. That mansion is called Goya's Grotto. E. Goísta built it, oh, fifteen years ago."

"Was that the mansion we saw on the way over here?" Juni asked. "The one that looked like a polka-dotted orange watermelon standing on one end?"

"That's the one!" Nana cried. "Ah, he's a genius, that Goísta!"

The spies exchanged more shifty looks. Then Dad put down his dessert spoon and cleared his throat.

"Tell me, Mama," he said. "You've lived in Madrid all your life. You must have seen E. Goísta somewhere. Maybe . . . outside the mansion where he lives?"

"Oh, no," Nana said, helping herself to Carmen's barely touched flan. "Nobody knows where E. Goísta lives, and nobody's ever seen him. He sends his blueprints out of his headquarters by messenger in the dead of night. He supervises his building projects from a helicopter. Very elusive, that E. Goísta. Even those of us who work for him have never met him."

"Those of *us*?" Dad blurted. "Mama! What are you talking about?"

"I wrote you that I was doing volunteer work," Nana said, licking a bit of caramel off her spoon. "I'm a docent at Goya's Grotto. I give tours to visitors."

"Oh," Dad said, with a confused scowl. He turned to his family and muttered under his breath, "If it is not one parent living a secret life, it's another!"

Mom put a soothing hand on Dad's shoulder and spoke to her mother-in-law.

"I think that's great, Mama!" she said. "Keeps you busy."

"Oh, *sí*," Nana said. "In fact, I have to give a tour tomorrow morning. I hope you can entertain yourselves while I work. Of course, I'll leave breakfast out for you before I leave."

Juni heaved a big sigh and exchanged relieved

glances with his parents and sister. Then he scooped the last bit of flan out of his custard cup and grinned at his grandmother.

"Nana," he said happily, "it's like you read our minds!"

CHAPTER 5

The next morning, the Cortezes left the house early, stopping only briefly in Nana's kitchen to gulp down some hot chocolate and cinnamon-sugary fried churros.

Then, they began walking toward Madrid's bustling downtown. They were dressed for action. Dad wore a sleek designer suit while Mom was decked out in a dress straight off the Paris runway. Their plan was to infiltrate Madrid's finest restaurants. They hoped to sniff out E. Goísta gobbling a gourmet meal in disguise.

Carmen and Juni, on the other hand, were dressed as . . . tacky tourists. Juni was wearing Dad's floppy hat, some baggy shorts, and black socks with sandals. Carmen had a camera around her neck and a bulging fanny pack clasped around her waist. They both wore stripes of white zinc oxide on their noses, as well as big sunglasses (secretly outfitted with telephoto lenses and spy cameras, of course).

Carmen carried the Madrid map that Devlin had sent them—the one that highlighted E. Goísta mansions all over the city.

"So, we're art history students doing a report on E. Goísta's architecture," Juni said to his parents. "We'll spend the day tromping from one building to another. And *you're* gourmands eating at Madrid's finest restaurants? No fair!"

"I promise to bring you a doggie bag," Mom said with a grin. She stopped walking to swipe an errant smear of zinc oxide off Juni's cheek. Then she gave him a kiss good-bye.

"Just hit every E. Goísta building you can," she said to the Spy Kids. "Look for trapdoors, secret chambers, two-way mirrors, anything that might lead us to the mad architect himself."

"Roger," Carmen said as Mom planted a kiss on top of her head, too. "We'll start near the Plaza Mayor. There's a big cluster of Goístas there."

"Remember, children," Dad said, "keep your eyes open. And stay in contact with us through your spy watches."

Then Dad turned to offer Mom his arm.

"And now, Ingrid," he said, "let's eat!"

Juni gave his father a baleful glare.

"Er," Dad said quickly, "let's *spy*, I mean. It will

be very hard work—right, my darling?"

"Huh," Juni grumbled as he and Carmen began to walk toward the plaza. He stomped down the sidewalk. "No fair . . . who's the chef in the family, anyway?"

Carmen rolled her eyes and gave Juni a little shove.

"Are you gonna spend the day complaining or spying?" she asked. "Or maybe you think your stomach's more important than the fate of Madrid's entire population?"

Juni looked sheepish.

"'Course not," he said. "But as we both know, I always spy better on a full stomach."

"Yeah—which I guess is why you ate about a dozen churros at breakfast this morning," Carmen sputtered. Suddenly, she pointed to an open area about a block away from them.

"There's the Plaza Mayor," she said. It was a grand square surrounded by stately stone-colored buildings and a few Goístas that stuck out like sore thumbs. One resembled a bright blue, transparent aquarium. Another looked like a cone-shaped, polka-dotted flamenco dancer's skirt. And another looked like a tubular water slide tied into knots.

The sprawling plaza before these buildings

bustled with businesspeople walking to work, retirees sipping coffee at outdoor cafés, buskers and street artists, and lots of tourists who looked just like Carmen and Juni.

"Looks like we're in the right place," Carmen murmured. "And our costumes certainly fit in. . . ."

As she surveyed the scene, Carmen noticed a mime standing on the sidewalk about ten feet away. Naturally, he was pretending to climb an invisible wall. And naturally, every passerby was ignoring him.

But in other ways, this mime was unusual. Instead of wearing a black bodysuit, he was dressed in about a million different colors. And he had the longest legs Carmen had ever seen. They seemed to sprout from his squat torso like sunflower stalks.

"Juni," Carmen whispered. "Do you think there's anything fishy about that mi—Juni? Juni?!"

Carmen had been so immersed in her spying, she hadn't realized that Juni was not beside her. Or behind her. Or in front of her! Carmen spun around and scanned the busy sidewalk frantically.

"Juni!" she shouted desperately.

"Whathup?" said a garbled voice right behind her. Carmen spun back around to find Juni blinking at her innocently. He had a dollop of chocolate on his lip and a half-eaten, gloppy crepe in one hand. He'd spoken with his mouth full, as usual.

"Don't sneak off like that!" Carmen said. "We're on a mission, remember?"

"All I did was get a snack from a street vendor," Juni complained. He took another big bite of his crepe as he and Carmen walked into the Plaza Mayor. "All that food talk made me hung—*whoa*!"

Juni squealed as his toe—in his big, tacky tourist sandal—hit a cobblestone in the sidewalk. He went flying. And so did his crepe!

"Oooooff," Juni grunted as he hit the sidewalk, right on his belly.

Splaaat! went the crepe as it landed about ten feet away, right in the middle of a chalk drawing of the aquarium-shaped Goísta.

A . . . half-finished chalk drawing.

Sitting next to the splattered crepe and ruined drawing was a street artist who'd clearly been hard at work when the flying dessert had made its unexpected appearance. This street artist was as odd-looking as the mime. His pumpkin-colored hair was arranged into a sort of lopsided curlicue. In fact, the man's hair looked a lot like one of the swirly flourishes on an E. Goísta building.

Beneath that odd hairdo was a furious scowl.

And the blue chalk in the artist's clenched fist was quickly turning to dust.

"Cretin!" he yelled at Juni. "You have ruined my drawing! So I will ruin *you!*"

"Uh-oh," Carmen said. "Juni—run!"

The Spy Kids turned on their heels and began tearing back down the busy street, away from the Plaza Mayor. As Juni dashed down the sidewalk, he heard something whistle past his ear.

He's shooting at us, Juni thought desperately. Just as he was about to dive for cover, something connected with his neck. It stung sharply. Juni yelped. He was hit!

As he continued running, Juni slapped his hand over the wound. But when he looked down at his palm, there was no blood. Only an orange, dusty powder.

"He's beaming us with sidewalk chalk!" Juni huffed to Carmen, who was running alongside him.

"I know! *Ow!*" she squealed. A bit of purple chalk had just nicked her ear. "We've got to lose this guy. We don't have time for this!"

The Spy Kids ducked around corners and dove behind sidewalk café tables. But every time they poked their heads out of their hiding places, the angry artist was still on their tail. Finally, the kids dashed into an alley and hid at the end of a long row of trash cans. The artist followed after them and began kicking the metal bins out of the way, one by one.

"He's determined!" Juni huffed as they crouched out of sight. "Sheesh, I wonder how he reacts when it rains and his precious drawings disappear altogether?!"

"Hmmm," Carmen mused. "That gives me an idea."

She unzipped her fanny pack and searched through it. Finally, she pulled out a tiny box with a joystick jutting out of it.

"Is that a Floodgate 2000?" Juni said.

"An old model, but it still works!" Carmen said with a grin. "Let's see if we can turn this chase around."

Carmen held the box out in front of her and hit a blue button next to the joystick. Some wispy, white vapor began to ooze out of the box. Before long, the vapor had formed a fluffy cloud that rose into the air.

Carmen waggled the joystick, and the cloud began to move.

"It's working!" Juni giggled under his breath.

Carmen steered the bouncing cloud over the

head of the artist, who was still searching for the Spy Kids. He took no notice of the fluffy cloud that was suddenly hovering right over his head. That is, until, Carmen hit the blue button on the Floodgate 2000.

Splaassssh!

The cloud broke apart like an eggshell. Great torrents of water began pouring down upon the vengeful artist's head.

"*Aigh!*" the shocked villain shrieked. As his curlicue of orange hair flattened against his pale skull, he gaped up at the cloud, a cloud that was raining down on him alone.

"What is this?" he cried in confusion. He stumbled to the left.

Carmen steered the cloud left.

He staggered to the right.

Carmen steered the cloud right.

Then the artist began running in panicky circles around the alley. But the cloud still followed him.

Finally, he yelled, "Ah, I give up!"

Carmen gave Juni a wink and pressed a red button on the Floodgate 2000. The cloud clammed up as quickly as it had opened. The tremendous rain shower died away. But just in case, Carmen kept the cloud hovering threateningly, just over the artist's head.

The man glared around the alley, trying to see Carmen and Juni through his dripping orange eyebrows. But when the two remained hidden and silent behind the trash bins, he waved dismissively.

"Kids!" he said as he stomped out of the alley.

Carmen was in the middle of a triumphant grin when something made her start.

"Soon you'll be fast asleep like everyone else," the artist mumbled as he walked away.

Carmen gasped.

"Did you hear that?" she whispered to Juni. "He knows about E. Goísta's plan. Which means he's *in* on the plan. We have to catch him!"

CHAPTER 6

Carmen and Juni dashed out of the alley and scanned the sidewalk for the suspicious street artist.

"There he is!" Juni cried, pointing to a damp curlicue of pumpkin-colored hair bobbing through the throngs of people.

The Spy Kids began dodging and weaving through the crowd. But the foot traffic was brutal. Everywhere they turned, they were blocked by camera-wielding tourists or newspaper-toting commuters.

"We're totally going to lose him!" Juni cried.

"Oh, no, we're not," Carmen replied. She gritted her teeth and tapped the big, rubbery toes of her sneakers on the pavement. With a loud *sproing*, a full set of Rollerblade wheels popped out of the soles.

Then she unzipped the pouch on her fanny pack and swung it around her waist until it rested on the small of her back. She punched a button on the fanny-pack strap. A tiny—but powerful—propeller shot out of the pouch.

"Pop out your own wheels!" Carmen ordered her brother. Automatically, Juni tapped his sandaled toes on the ground, unleashing his own set of instant Rollerblades.

Carmen grabbed his shirt collar and pressed another button on her strap. The propeller sputtered into action, and the Spy Kids took off. They hopped the curb and began zipping along the edge of the street with the speed of a small plane.

"Now, this is how to travel!" Juni said.

"Be careful," Carmen warned. "You know Mom and Dad hate when we don't go the regulated speed limit."

"There he is," Juni cried, pointing at the gated entrance to a large park. The kids saw the orange curlicue pass through the gate. But between them and their prey were dozens of milling people.

"How are we going to get through this crowd?" Juni wondered.

"Hang on!" Carmen answered.

She tightened her grip on her brother's shirt collar.

Then she jumped.

"Aaaaaahhh!" Juni shrieked as the propeller sent them hurtling into the air. The Spy Kids made a long, lazy arc over the sidewalk full of people, landing just behind the artist with a *thwap!*

"Gotcha!" Carmen said. She released Juni's collar and pounced upon the pumpkin-colored curlicue. She grabbed the villain from behind, and together Spy Kid and street artist tumbled to the grass.

But when the villain cried out, his voice had changed. It was shriller. And higher. And . . . female.

"Huh?" Carmen exclaimed in confusion. She grabbed the artist, who was sprawled on her stomach, and flipped her over. Then she gasped.

This was not their street artist.

This wasn't even a man!

In fact, it was a well-heeled woman in a fuzzy, orange, curlicue-shaped hat.

"Mugger!" the woman shrieked. "Police! Help me! This hooligan is trying to steal my purse!"

"Am not!" Carmen gasped in Spanish. "This is just a case of mistaken identity. Sorry, ma'am!"

"Police!" the woman shrieked again, clutching her purse to her chest. "Help!"

Juni skated over and grabbed Carmen's elbow.

"She's serious," he hissed. "If the police come, we'll lose valuable time. We've gotta dash."

Carmen stumbled to her feet.

"*¡Perdón, perdón!*" she said to the woman, but the lady wasn't having it. She continued to shriek and point at Carmen with an accusing, red long-nailed finger.

So Carmen shrugged, grabbed Juni's collar once again, and turned her propeller back on.

"Off we goooooo!" Juni cried as they zoomed off into the park. They raced down paths and around hedges until, finally, they collapsed behind a fountain in a small courtyard.

"Nobody's going to catch us now," Carmen said, tapping on her sneaker toes to retract her Rollerblade wheels.

"Yeah, but we're not going to catch that evil sidewalk artist, either," Juni said with a pout. "We're no closer to finding E. Goísta than we were before!"

Carmen hung her head and sighed. Juni was right. They were getting nowhere fast—even with their power jet Rollerblades.

Twang-strum-strum-strum.

Carmen's ears perked up.

"Listen to that," she said to Juni. "It's a Spanish guitar." The tune that suddenly filled the air was so beautiful, it was almost impossible for her to stay upset.

"Where's it coming from?" Carmen wondered.

"Sounds like it's on the other side of that hedge over there," Juni said, pointing to a tall leafy shrub that bordered the courtyard. The Spy Kids got to their feet and walked over to the hedge, peeking around it. Sure enough, a busker was sitting at the edge of a walking path. He was plucking his guitar with amazing skill and grace. Several passersby dropped pesetas into the open guitar case at the musician's feet.

"I've never heard anyone play like that!" Carmen breathed. "He's amazing."

"Uh, Carmen?" Juni said.

"Shhhh," Carmen said, holding up her hand. "He's almost at the end of the song."

"Listen . . . I think I know why he's so great," Juni said nervously.

"Hmmmm," Carmen replied absently.

"Count the fingers," Juni whispered.

"What?" Carmen asked, glancing at her brother in irritation.

"Count . . . his . . . fingers," Juni hissed through gritted teeth.

As the musician continued to strum and pluck,

Carmen squinted at his left hand.

"Four, five," she muttered, "six, seven?!"

She gasped and glanced at Juni.

"He's got two extra fingers on each hand," she whispered.

"Uh-huh," Juni said. "And that sidewalk artist had a bizarro balding pattern." Juni stared at the leopard pattern of hair (and missing hair) on the freaky man.

As the Spy Kids pondered the strange street artists, the guitarist began another song. This one was so captivating, a small crowd of people stopped to listen.

"Come on," Carmen said. "Let's keep searching."

But Juni wouldn't move.

"Juni!" Carmen said. "I know the guitar's pretty, but this is no time for a music-appreciation moment."

Juni gave his sister a pointed look, then nodded subtly at one of the onlookers. The man was holding a straw bag brimming with an aged salami, a crusty loaf of bread, a wedge of yellow cheese, a bottle of expensive-looking wine, and other mouthwatering foodstuffs.

"It's not time for a snack, either!" Carmen said. "You and your munchies. That's what got us into this mess in the first place."

"Take a closer look," Juni said, slyly adjusting his telephoto sunglasses.

Carmen sighed and toggled her own sunglasses. She fiddled with one arm of the glasses until her line of vision zoomed forward. She honed in on the man with the shopping bag.

His eyes were shifty.

His mouth was screwed into a smug frown.

His baggy shirt was smudged with brightly colored paint.

And beneath his spiky, bleached hair and black beret was one . . . two . . . *three* ears!

Carmen gulped and turned to Juni.

"Another mutant artist," she whispered.

"With a bag of gourmet food," Juni replied. "Now, what starving artist do you know who can afford that kind of grub?"

"Maybe it's for E. Goísta!" Carmen whispered.

"Exactly," Juni said. "Let's tail this guy."

No sooner had the words left his mouth than the painter made to leave. He gave the guitarist a knowing look, then turned on his heel and began walking out of the park.

The painter began to hurry through Madrid's narrow, quaint streets. He rushed past cafés and apartment buildings. He also whisked by several garish Goístas, but he didn't give even them a glance.

Clearly, this man was on a mission.

And Carmen and Juni were at their spying best. They skittered a half block behind the food-laden artist, ducking behind lampposts, churro stands, and parked cars. Their prey didn't suspect a thing.

Finally, he came to a halt in front of an enormous cathedral.

"It's the Basílica Bombardo," Carmen whispered, glancing at Devlin's map. "E. Goísta's biggest and gaudiest creation."

"You said it!" Juni breathed. He gaped up at the church's long, curly spires. They extended into the sky like twisty-turny balloon animals. The spires framed a big, soap-bubble-like, glass dome. The church's stained-glass windows came in every shape and size, and no two were alike. The grand staircase was dotted with bright polka dots. And the front doors were shaped like circles, squares, triangles, and one hexagon.

In fact, the painter with the foodstuffs was slipping through the hexagon at that moment.

"All right," Juni said, tweaking his tacky tourist hat with determination. "We're going in!"

The Spy Kids ran up the church steps and walked through the geometric door. They gazed wildly around the cathedral.

It was an enormous, open space encircled by candy-striped columns. The ceiling was painted with a vast, brightly colored scene of animals and angels scampering through the heavens. In the middle of the painting, the looming, glass dome refracted the sunlight into a thousand little round rainbows.

Meanwhile, down on the rainbow-tiled floor, there were dozens of pews. Each was made of a different material—from purple-enameled copper to cherry-stained wood to pale orange marble.

There was so much to look at, it made the Spy Kids' eyes go buggy.

But the one thing they *didn't* see in the eerily quiet sanctuary was the painter!

"Where'd he go?!" Carmen whispered.

"I don't know," Juni said, dashing down the aisle to peek under pews and peer around columns. "It's like he disappeared into thin air . . . hmmmm."

Juni's voice trailed off as he stared up at the enormous fresco on the ceiling.

"What?" Carmen said, glancing upward as well.

"There's something about that painting. . . ."

Juni mused. Then, without another word, he dug into a pocket of his baggy shorts. He pulled out a bright blue ball and popped it into his mouth.

"What are you snacking on now?" Carmen demanded.

"It's not a snack," Juni said. "It's an Uncle Machete gizmo—a Huffenpuff Hot Air Pill."

"What?" Carmen demanded. "No hoarding the gadgets, Juni! Hand one of those pills over."

Then Juni's face screwed up into a disgusted grimace.

"Ugh!" he said. "It tastes like hot, melted crayons!"

"Oh, uh, never mind then! It's all yours, bro," Carmen said with a nervous laugh. "What's it do, anyway?"

Before Juni could answer, his feet began to rise off the cathedral floor. They hovered a few inches off the ground for a moment before rising a few inches more.

"Juni!" Carmen gasped. "You're floating!"

By now, Juni's tacky, sandaled feet were hovering a foot off the ground. And then two feet, three feet . . .

In another instant, he was soaring toward the ceiling like a hot-air balloon.

"Whoo-hoo!" Juni said, waving at Carmen as he floated off. "It's working!"

"But where are you *going*?" Carmen demanded. By now, all she could see were the soles of Juni's sandals, kicking wildly as he flew up, up, up. Carmen saw him gaze down at her and open his mouth to answer.

But before he could utter a word, he had disappeared!

CHAPTER 7

"Juni!" Carmen screamed. She turned around in a circle. And then gazed up. "Where'd you go?!?"

There was no answer. Carmen's voice merely echoed against the walls of the empty cathedral.

In confusion, Carmen scanned the ceiling again. But all she could see was the goofy fresco. And the glass dome. And . . . a little plaster lip! There was a ledge where the ceiling met the base of the dome!

Carmen put on her telephoto sunglasses and squinted at the shallow ledge close-up.

"The ledge is approximately four inches wide and composed of steel-enforced plaster," Carmen muttered to herself. "No problem."

With that, she unzipped her fanny pack and pulled out her trusty Claw 'n' Cable. All she had to do was throw the claw up to the ledge, get a secure hold, and shinny up the superstrong cable.

And then she'd track down her brother.

Carmen gripped the claw in her right hand, took careful aim, and then tossed it toward the dome. Her aim—honed in countless hours of spy training—was perfect. The claw was precisely positioned to connect with the ledge. With grim satisfaction, Carmen waited for the claw's pointed ends to grip the ledge's surface, and then for the cable to go taut.

But that didn't happen.

Instead, the claw's points seemed to slice right through the ledge! Without leaving even a tiny mark.

Just as Carmen unleashed a bewildered little squeal, her spy watch sputtered to life.

"Carmen!" said a muffled voice.

Carmen sighed in relief and pushed the intercom button on her watch.

"Juni!" she huffed. "Where are you?"

"My suspicions were right on!" her brother's triumphant voice said.

"And those suspicions were what, exactly?" Carmen said.

"The fresco," Juni replied through the watch. "It's false—a hologram or high-tech optical illusion. I sailed right through it. As I entered, it made a really cool, gross, squelching noise!"

"Just like my Claw 'n' Cable," Carmen said. "But where are you now?"

"I hit a trapdoor and climbed through," Juni replied. "I'm in this huge apartment. It's *gotta* be E. Goísta's."

Carmen slumped into one of the artsy pews. It was hard and uncomfortable, which completely suited her mood.

"How do you know it's E. Goísta's?" she said into her watch nervously.

"How many people do you know who decorate their living rooms with huge gold and silver polka dots and curlicues and nothing but beanbag chairs?" Juni replied. "Besides, I can also smell about a million fabulous foods cooking up here. Yum!"

"So, now what?" Carmen said, rolling her eyes as she heard Juni smacking his lips through her intercom.

"I'll do some reconnaissance," Juni replied. "And you can get in touch with Mom and Dad and tell them the latest. I'll get you guys some intel as soon as I can. Over and out."

With another sputter, Carmen's spy watch went silent. She gazed at it irritably.

First, Juni hoards away his Huffenpuff Hot Air Pills and floats away without a word, thought Carmen. Then he discovers E. Goísta—alone! Meanwhile, I'm just a messenger girl. I've heard of too many cooks spoiling the broth, but ditching your spy partner? That is uncool!

Wow! Juni thought as he clicked off his spy watch's intercom. I've infiltrated E. Goísta's secret headquarters!

He looked warily around the garish room. It suddenly looked very big. And foreboding. And . . . empty. And Juni couldn't help but wonder what Carmen would suggest if she were there.

But Carmen wasn't there. Juni was just going to have to go it alone.

I can do it, he told himself as he crept through the huge gold-and-silver living room. And I *will* do it. I'll scour these church-top chambers, evade E. Goísta's creepy minions, and *find* that evil architect, no matter what it takes. I will sniff him out . . . sniff him . . . sniff . . . hmmm, that food smells really good!

"Ah!" Juni breathed as he took another deep whiff of the air. "I think I detect notes of prawns simmering in garlic, and spicy *patatas bravas* and . . . is that *dulce de leche* I smell?"

Juni half-closed his eyes as the smell of warm caramel filled his nose. Then he drifted toward a door at the far end of the living room. And before he knew what he was doing, he'd plunged through the door into the most fabulous kitchen he'd ever seen!

There was an eight-burner professional range.

There was a cold, marble pastry counter.

A stainless steel Sub-Zero refrigerator.

Even a family-size George Foreman grill!

And, bubbling on one of the stove's burners was, indeed, a saucepan filled with fragrant, bubbling *dulce de leche*.

Juni looked around the warm, mammoth kitchen.

There was not a soul to be seen.

"Just one little taste," Juni whispered to himself. "And *then* I'll look for E. Goísta. . . ."

He grabbed a spoon from a jar on the counter and dipped it into the pot of gooey, sugary caramel. Then he licked the sticky spoon clean of the delicious molten candy.

"Magnífica!" he whispered.

But before Juni truly had a chance to savor the sweet stuff, a voice rang out behind him!

"Intruder!"

"Huh?" Juni squeaked. He spun around to face the pantry. Emerging from the closet was a cook with a wild mop of gray hair and a huge, floppy white hat. His chef's uniform was just E. Goísta's style. The pants billowed out like baggy jodhpurs. And the smock was decorated with grafitti in ketchup red, egg yolk–yellow and egg-plant purple.

The cook glowered at Juni from beneath fluffy, silver eyebrows. Then he began to run across the tiled kitchen floor. The man did not look like he was too happy. In fact, he looked downright mad. He was waving a very large whisk.

Clearly, he wasn't afraid to use it.

Juni felt his forehead break out in beads of cold sweat.

What do I do now? he thought desperately.

But an instant later, his training kicked in. He suddenly remembered the cardinal rule of spying: when you've been caught; when gadgetry isn't at your fingertips; and when your strength is out-weighed—improvise!

And so, an instant before the attack-cook brought his whisk crashing down upon Juni's head, the Spy Kid held up his hand.

"Halt!" he ordered the cook in perfectly accented Spanish. "What do you think you're doing with that whisk, young man?"

"*Young* man?" the cook gasped, gazing down at Juni incredulously.

"You are waving it around like a novice," Juni pronounced, "when what you *should* be doing is stirring this caramel."

In one deft move, Juni swiped the whisk out of the cook's hand and thunked it into the saucepan. Then he began stirring the caramel with brisk, confident strokes.

"Don't you know," Juni scolded, "if you don't stir *dulce de leche* constantly, it will scorch?"

Then Juni shook his fist and rolled his eyes.

"I am working with amateurs here!" he said to no one in particular.

"Ex-*cuse* me," the cook said haughtily, "but I am no amateur, sir. I was trained in Spain's most prestigious culinary school. I graduated at the top of my class. And who are *you*, short boy?"

"Who am I?" Juni sputtered with false arrogance. He puffed out his chest—well, his belly— and made his eyes bulge with false rage. "*Who am I? What an absolutely inane question.*"

Who *am* I? the Spy Kid thought, stirring the

caramel in panicky swirls. He looked around the kitchen desperately.

And in that kitchen, he found his answer—the perfect way to get at E. Goísta.

"I am Umberto Radicchio," he declared, "the new personal chef of Mr. E. Goísta!"

CHAPTER 8

Carmen squinted at the numbers fanned out in front of her.

C'mon, *think*, she scolded herself. You're a hacker. No mathematic permutation is beyond you. You can crack this code!

Finally, she took a stab at a solution.

"Do you have any . . . fours?" she asked.

"Go fish!" Nana cried.

"Blast!" Carmen said, throwing down her playing cards.

Nana chuckled kindly.

"I don't know how I win again," she said apologetically. "Beginner's luck, I guess."

"I guess," Carmen said, slumping back in her chair. "Congratulations, Nana."

"*Gracias, gracias,*" Nana said with another laugh. "Oh, I am so enjoying having you here. Too bad Juni isn't here. Isn't it funny that he ran into that distant Cortez cousin today in the city?"

"Uh, yeah," Carmen said. "And they became such good friends, they decided to have a sleepover!"

At least, she added inside her head, that's the story we told you, so that you wouldn't discover that your grandson, Juni, is a spy doing dangerous undercover work in the headquarters of a superevil architect!

Nana had bought the three Cortezes' story completely. And then, the spies had settled in for a night of waiting. There was nothing they could do until Juni sent them some intel through his spy watch.

So, at the moment, they were powerless.

Carmen cast a wary glance across Nana's cozy living room. Dad was lounging in a brown leather chair, pretending to read a travel book about Madrid. But he was really studying the blueprints of various E. Goísta buildings.

Mom was typing on her laptop, pretending to write in a travel diary. But she was really trying to hack into the Basílica Bombardo's Website to see if she could figure out another way into E. Goísta's headquarters.

And Carmen was pretending to enjoy playing Go Fish with her grandmother. But she was really seething. And it wasn't just because she was losing the game.

I can't believe Juni is saving the world—well, Madrid—without me, she thought. I feel so useless!

It didn't help that every time she stole to her room to check in with Juni through her spy watch, he was speaking in a code she couldn't understand. What was he talking about?

First, he'd reported: "The steak is sizzling."

"What'd you say?" Carmen replied into her spy watch. "Steak?"

"Roger that," Juni replied.

"But what does that mea—" Carmen began, but Juni clicked out before he could explain. Carmen had rolled her eyes and stomped out of her room. This was not her idea of a good time.

After the Go Fish game, Carmen checked in with her brother again.

"The tapas are tepid," he said this time. He sounded a bit dejected. And, of course, completely nonsensical.

"Hello," Carmen sputtered into her spy watch. "Listen, Mr. I've-Watched-Too-Many-Spy-Movies. If you're gonna speak in code, it helps to tell your partner that code *before* you head into the mission."

"Gotta go," Juni responded quickly. "The flan is flaming."

"Whatever," Carmen said. She clicked off her spy watch again. Irritably, she stomped down the short hallway that led from the bedrooms to the living room. When she arrived, Nana and her parents were having an argument.

"I insist upon it," Nana was saying. "This is Madrid—the city where you fell in love. You must go out on the town. Have some dinner, do a little dancing. You work too hard, you two!"

"Really, Mama," Mom said from her seat on the couch. She was fiddling nervously with her laptop. "We're perfectly content staying home with you and Carmen."

"Oh, pshaw," Nana said. "I want to have my granddaughter to myself for the evening. We've been having so much fun together. You two should take advantage and take some time for *your*selves. Get a jump on the *Dos de Mayo* festival! It starts tomorrow, you know. Today is May first!"

"What's Dos de Mayo?" Carmen piped up.

"That's right, we've never been here for that, have we?" Dad said to Carmen with a grin. "Dos de Mayo—or May the second—is like the Fourth of July in America. Instead of independence from the

British, however, the Spaniards celebrate their freedom from French rule. Our revolution began on May 2, 1808."

"And these days," Nana said, "it means a *big* party. The entire city takes to the streets! As should you, Ingrid and Gregorio!"

Mom and Dad shot Carmen desperate looks. But Carmen just shrugged.

"Nana's right," she admitted. "There's nothing more you can do here. And you'll have your pager with you, right? So, if Juni calls—"

Carmen gave her Nana a quick, careful glance.

"To, uh, say good night or anything like that," she continued, "I'll page you. I've got it covered."

"I suppose you are right, Carmenita," Dad said with a worried grimace.

"Yes, a couple of hours in the city shouldn't do any harm," Mom said with a nervous shrug.

"Go, go," Nana said, waving away her son and daughter-in-law with a laugh. "Have yourselves a good time."

And so they did.

A couple of hours later, Carmen was slumped on the couch in a heavy-lidded pout.

Mom and Dad were out dancing.

Nana was snoring gently in the chair where she'd dozed off.

And Carmen's spy watch was crackling. Juni was logging in for another annoyingly encrypted report.

"The pork chops are tasty," he said through the watch.

"Oh, how very helpful, Juni," Carmen muttered dryly. She felt her eyelids drop another notch. She glanced at Nana's sleeping form. Then she looked at the clock, tick-tick-ticking the minutes away. Through a weary haze, she heard Juni's voice echo out of the spy watch one more time.

"I repeat, the pork chops are extremely tasty," Juni said.

"Whatever . . ." Carmen whispered. Then her eyes closed completely and she fell fast asleep.

Juni was crouched in the pantry of E. Goísta's enormous, humming kitchen, whispering into his spy watch.

"I repeat," he said, "the pork chops are extremely tasty."

Then he pressed the watch's RECEIVE button to catch Carmen's reply.

"*Rraaaawwrrr!*" his sister said.

"Didn't quite catch that," Juni whispered into

his watch. "Was that a yawn? Over."

But all Juni got in reply was sleepy silence.

"Whatever," Juni muttered, as he got to his feet and grabbed a few onions out of the root bin. He smoothed down his baggy, checkered chef's pants and colorful smock. (He'd grabbed them from a utility closet earlier and changed out of his tacky tourist disguise.) Then Juni put on his game face—a haughty sneer—and stalked back into the kitchen. The room was now bustling with cooks getting an enormous feast ready for E. Goísta.

"You, there," Juni ordered, pointing to a cook standing in front of a large range. "Stir that sauce. It's going to curdle."

Then he peeked around the elbow of another cook who was chopping vegetables. He snatched a wafer-thin slice of carrot from the woman's work area. Holding up the carrot, Juni examined the slice.

"You must slice thinner," Juni said. "I should be able to *see through* these vegetables."

He tossed the carrot back into the pile with a sniff.

"I will present only the best to E. Goísta," he announced to the room. "After all, when I serve the great architect his dinner, I don't want to be embarrassed by fat carrots."

Suddenly, the activity in the kitchen ground to a halt. All chatter ceased. The bubbling of gravy, the simmering of stew, and the hum of the rotisserie skewered with juicy spring chickens became eerily loud.

"What?" Juni said edgily. "Something I said?"

"You said *you* would be serving E. Goísta personally," one of the cooks piped up. "But, Chef Radicchio, none of us has ever *seen* E. Goísta in person. He is a famous hermit, after all. The only people he will let near him are his fellow artists. All others are shunned."

"I . . . know that!" Juni sputtered, thrusting a finger in the air. "I was . . . just testing you, of course. Back to work!"

Juni clapped his hands and stalked over to the oven, pretending it was time to check on the pork chops.

Okay, E. Goísta is off-limits, he thought shakily. Time for Plan B. Now, if I only knew what Plan B was. . . .

As his mind spun desperately, Juni whipped the tray of pork chops out of the oven and took a taste. They were done.

At least there was one thing I wasn't lying about, he mumbled to himself. The pork chops really *are* extremely tasty.

As Juni tried to come up with a scheme, he found himself squinting at the long bones of the pork chops. The bones were bare, serving as little more than handles for hungry diners. They poked up over the ends of the tray like little flagpoles.

As Juni stared at the bones, he suddenly smiled.

Aha, he thought, snapping his fingers. This was going to be the perfect Plan B. Spying was in Juni's bones!

CHAPTER 9

A few minutes later, a voice rang out through E. Goísta's kitchen: "Dinner is served!"

Juni looked around for the source of the voice. Finally, he realized that someone was yelling through a small door in the wall. Juni had thought it was a cupboard. Instead, it was a window leading into the dining room. And in that dining room the evil E. Goísta sat, waiting to be fed his supper feast.

Juni gave his pork chops one last once-over. He squinted carefully at each of the chop bones. The supertiny, fish-eye video cameras he'd glued to the bones were almost invisible. Yes!

Then Juni pressed a button on his spy watch. A staticky image appeared on the watch's tiny screen. It was the kitchen floor.

Juni pushed the button again. This time, he saw the kitchen counter, littered with carrot tops and potato peelings. When he pressed the button again, he saw his own, stressed-out face.

All right, Juni thought. Every camera is working and relaying its image back to my spy watch. With these chops, I should get at least one good shot of E. Goísta. More important, my audio feed will clue me in on his plan!

Juni crossed his fingers and silently added, I hope!

He swept up the tray of pork chops and marched it over to the window. A pair of hands was thrust through the opening, waiting to whisk away one of the dinner dishes. Just before Juni placed his tray into the hands, he gasped.

Each of the hands sported seven fingers! It was the guitarist from the park!

That proves it, Juni thought triumphantly as the mutated hands whisked the tray away. Every strange street artist we've seen around Madrid must be a minion of E. Goísta! He's got a virtual army milling around this city! His "people" were everywhere! They must be part of the plan!

Of course, Juni still had to find out what that plan was!

When all the dinner dishes had finally been sent into the dining room, Juni pointed to one of the cooks.

"You," he barked. "Start melting some bittersweet

chocolate for dessert. And don't burn it!"

"Yes, Chef Radicchio!" the cowed cook cried. He rushed to hack a hunk of chocolate from a deep-brown brick in the pantry.

"And you!" Juni said to another cook slaving over a bowl of fluffy white stuff. "Make that whipped cream whippier!"

"Sí, chef!" the cook cried.

Finally, Juni dusted off his hands and declared loudly, "I am taking a well-deserved coffee break. I do not wish to be disturbed!"

"Yes, Chef Radicchio," all the cooks said together.

Juni stalked out of the kitchen, back to the gold-and-silver living room. He flopped into a beanbag chair and began pushing the audio-video-input button on his spy watch. He held his breath as image after image flashed onto the watch's tiny screen.

First, he saw the fourteen-fingered guitarist, arranging food on the table. Then he spotted the man with the orange, curlicued hair! He was pouring wine. Next, Juni saw a row of empty, high-backed, crazily decorated dining room chairs. And finally, at a funny angle, he saw a man who had to be seen to be believed.

His hair was shimmery and powder blue. It was

waxed into tremendous billowy curls, swirls, and whorls. His mustache, which was lemon yellow, hung in corkscrews upon his plump cheeks.

His enormously fat torso was draped in a brightly colored silk and velvet vest. And tucked into his collar was a napkin of such grandeur, it might have been an antique tapestry. It was edged in golden fringe and decorated with a hand-painted image of a building that Juni thought he recognized.

"That's Goya's Grotto!" Juni suddenly realized. "And that's definitely E. Goísta! Ew!"

At the moment, the evil architect was silent, except for a lot of disgusting slurps, gargles, and snorts as he scarfed down the gourmet delights that covered the table.

"Mmmm," E. Goísta grunted in a guttural voice. "Pass me another hen, minion. Excellent . . . excellent . . ."

Juni's lip curled.

And Carmen thinks *I'm* a pig, he thought in disgust. If only she could get a load of this dude. He's a monster!

The thought gave Juni a little stab of loneliness. He suddenly realized how much cooler spying was when he had a partner. Even if that partner *was* his sister.

I should have shared my Huffenpuff Hot Air Pills with Carmen, he thought guiltily. If I had, I wouldn't be on this mission solo.

But before Juni had a chance to get really glum, something on his spy watch screen shook him out of his pity party. Another minion had entered the dining room and shuffled up next to E. Goísta's chair. This one was a clown with red and blue stripes on his face that somehow *didn't* look like makeup.

"Master Goísta, sir?" the clown said in a tremulous voice.

The fleshy villain glared at the clown through beady, bright green eyes.

"CAN'T YOU SEE I'M EATING!" E. Goísta bellowed.

"I beg your pardon, sir," the clown yelped. "I would never disturb your supper if it wasn't an emergency. You see, we've discovered something terrible. The OSS is on to us!"

Juni gulped!

And E. Goísta did something then that made every minion in the dining room gasp.

He stopped chewing.

Then he swiveled his big, wobbly neck and looked at the clown directly.

"Have they sent in the big guns?" E. Goísta inquired.

"*Sí*, Master Goísta," the clown replied. "The Cortez family."

Juni gulped a second time. E. Goísta knew all about his family! At the same time that Juni felt an instant pride about the Cortez reputation, he also experienced a quiver of fear. E. Goísta was more than mad. He was also smart! And that meant he was very dangerous.

The clown gave E. Goísta a sheaf of black-and-white photos. Juni toggled the button on his spy watch so that his pork-chop cam could zoom in. Then he gasped. The architect was looking at a picture of his family getting into the taxi at the airport. And there was a photo of Nana kissing Dad on the cheek. *And* a still wet picture of him and Carmen Rollerblading down the sidewalk! Juni did not expect to find the Cortez family vacation album here in E. Goísta's home!

I can't believe the whole time we were spying on E. Goísta, his minions were spying on us, Juni thought. The nerve!

E. Goísta's next statement was even more shocking to Juni.

"It is just as I expected," the evil architect said.

He resumed his gluttony by tearing a huge hunk of bread off a loaf at his elbow.

"Huh?" Juni gulped.

"Huh?" E. Goísta's minions gasped.

"What, did you think such a brilliant plan would go *completely* undetected?" E. Goísta said to his minions. "After all, I have spent decades building my architectural empire for this sole purpose."

"To attract the scrutiny of OSS spies?" asked the befuddled clown.

"No!" E. Goísta bellowed. "To lull all of Madrid to sleep. That will teach them to take my art for granted!

"The Madrileños have never appreciated us, my fellow artists," E. Goísta continued. He shook his meaty fist, which was clutching an enormous fork, in the air. "They ignore your mime routines and sidewalk drawings. They deign to *live* in my beautiful mansions.

"We are underappreciated," E. Goísta ranted on. "And underpaid! And, occasionally, even laughed at! And for this indignity, the Madrileños will pay!"

"*Sí, sí!*" every mutant painter, mime, and clown in the room cried.

"And they will pay when they are happiest,"

E. Goísta added. His lips curled into a fiendish grin. "During the celebration of the Dos de Mayo festival!"

"Dos de Mayo?" Juni whispered with a gulp. "That means May second. As in—tomorrow!"

"Yes, during Dos de Mayo," E. Goísta said, rubbing his oily palms together fiendishly, "one of my artists will station himself at every E. Goísta building in Madrid. Then, precisely at midnight . . ."

"We hit the buttons!" the artists shouted.

"You hit the buttons!" E. Goísta confirmed. "The buttons that I have hidden in every building I've ever built. The buttons that will release clouds of sleeping gas all over the city! Only those in gas masks—that is, us—will stay awake. And then, we will fill the city with art. Nobody will ever take our work for granted again!"

"Yay!" the artists cried.

"Yay!" Juni quietly echoed. "I know the plan! And the solution is so simple. All we have to do is intercept a minion at every E. Goísta building and prevent him from pushing that button!"

Juni was just getting ready to broadcast this intel to Carmen when E. Goísta spoke again. And this time, his gurgly voice sounded more sinister, more threatening, more gruesome than before. Juni paused and felt the hairs on his neck stand on end.

"My plan should go off without a hitch," Goísta said with a greasy grin. "Especially since we will have Juanita Cortez in our custody!"

"Nana?!" Juni gasped.

"With Mrs. Cortez's life in our hands," E. Goísta cackled, "we can count on her family to stay out of our way! Ah-ha-ha-ha!"

CHAPTER 10

As E. Goísta's maniacal laughter echoed out of Juni's spy watch, the Spy Kid slumped off his silver beanbag chair. He couldn't believe it. E. Goísta was going to kidnap his grandmother!

Juni didn't have a second to lose. He switched his spy watch's frequency back to Carmen's wavelength and started talking.

"Carmen!" he cried. "Big trouble! E. Goísta is planning on kidnapping Nana! You've got to keep an eye on her at all times!"

"*Plus,* you and Mom and Dad have got to make sure none of those street artists gets close to any E. Goísta buildings. They're going to hit a button during the Dos de Mayo celebration and unleash the sleeping gas all over Madrid."

"*Meanwhile,* I'm going to try to take out E. Goísta from the inside. Okay—got that?"

By the time Juni finished his orders, his face was purple and he was gasping for oxygen. He finally drew in a breath as he pressed his audio-input button. He braced himself for Carmen's cries of alarm and panic, followed by determined avowals to save the day.

But what he got was . . . silence, complete silence.

"Uh . . . Carmen?" Juni whispered.

Nothing.

Juni felt his eyes bulge as he switched frequencies and tried his parents' pager. Like Carmen's and Juni's spy watches, his parents' pager never left their side. Their response, he was sure, would be almost instantaneous.

Juni waited.

And waited.

When five minutes had gone by, Juni slapped his forehead and jumped to his feet.

"Where are they?" he wondered. Then he began stalking back to the kitchen.

"Looks like I'll have to cook up a plan all by myself," he groaned.

Meanwhile, Gregorio and Ingrid Cortez were sitting in the golden-lit outdoor courtyard of their favorite restaurant: the place they went to every time they were in Madrid—the place where they had fallen in love many years ago.

They were nibbling on olives with crusty bread and sipping sangria—fruity red wine dotted with bits of apples, oranges, and pears.

They were tapping their toes to the subtle strains of guitar and violin wafting over from a small bandstand at the courtyard's edge.

And every thirty seconds or so, one of the parents glanced nervously at their pager, which was propped against the candelabra so to be sure to hear it if someone were needed.

Neither was having very much fun.

"I feel so guilty," Mom said. "Here we are, out on the town while our son is risking life and limb on a mission."

"I know," Dad said, hanging his head for a moment. "And we wouldn't even be here if we didn't have to protect my mother from the truth. I am sorry, Ingrid."

Mom smiled at her husband wanly.

"It's not that I don't trust that Juni can handle himself," she added. "He'll do great, I know!"

"Of course he will," Dad agreed, thumping the table with his fist for emphasis. "We've raised a very savvy spy, my dear."

"Two of them!" Mom agreed. She flashed a

genuine grin for the first time that night. Suddenly—as if in answer—the band struck up a more raucous tune.

A flamenco tune.

"Tell you what," Dad said, getting to his feet and extending a hand toward his wife. "Give me this flamenco, and then we'll head home to wait for word from Juni with Carmen."

"Why, I'd love to, kind sir," Mom said, batting her eyelashes and getting up as well.

"You know if Carmen and Juni were here," Dad said, "what they would say . . . ?"

"'No mushy stuff!'" Mom laughed. "C'mon, let's dance." The tall, brown-eyed Spaniard and his slender, flame-haired wife stalked onto the dance floor. The couple faced each other, placed their hands on their hips, and stomped their feet. Then, they began to whirl around the dance floor.

Dad spun Mom this way and that. They stalked back and forth, cheek to cheek. They swirled in dizzying circles. And finally, Dad swung Mom into a deep, dramatic dip. When the Cortez parents righted themselves with a bold flourish of their wrists, every other diner in the restaurant burst into applause. Some even threw roses at Mom's feet.

The couple gave a gracious bow, then returned

to their small table in the courtyard.

"Well, that *did* make me feel better!" Mom said breathlessly.

"Yes, and we made it through the entire flamenco without a page from the children," Dad added. He popped an olive into his mouth and added, "Our kids can take care of themselves, eh, Ingrid? Ingrid?"

But Mom wasn't answering. In fact, her face had gone pale. And she was pointing into her goblet of sangria with a trembling finger.

Floating in the fruity wine was—their pager!

Their ruined pager.

Dad gasped and looked around the courtyard. His highly trained eyes immediately fell upon the most sinister-looking person in the restaurant—a strangely pale violinist on the bandstand. He was staring at the spies with a scowl. But as soon as Dad's eyes met his, the violinist threw his instrument to the ground and leaped off the stage. In an instant, he had melted into the crowd.

"Coward!" Dad roared. He jumped to his feet and started to chase the musician down. But before he could get far, Mom grabbed him.

"That guy doused our pager for one reason and one reason only," Mom gasped. "Because someone wants to get to our family. Let's check on them first. We'll deal with that scoundrel later."

"You are right, as always, Ingrid," Dad said in an anxious whisper. He threw a handful of pesetas onto their table and grabbed his wife's hand. Together, they ran out of the restaurant and back toward Nana's house.

The mayor of Madrid was addressing a crowd of several thousand Spaniards.

"In our city's long and distinguished history, we've never witnessed such heroism," he said. His voice boomed into the crowd with the aid of dozens of microphones, many of them belonging to international news crews. "I mean, sure, her little brother helped out, but really, we owe the salvation of Madrid to the renowned Spy Kid—Carmen Cortez!"

Carmen stepped to the podium and modestly waved to the roars of the crowd. She graciously accepted the key to the city from the mayor. She was just about to begin her brief yet profound speech, when suddenly, a voice jolted her.

"Carmen!"

Carmen looked up from the lectern. Who was calling her name?

"Carmen! Wake up!"

"Huh?"

Carmen's eyes fluttered open. The mayor and the throngs of grateful Madrileños melted away. In their place appeared the anxious faces of her mother and father, looming above her. Carmen jumped off the couch and rubbed her eyes.

"I . . . I must have fallen asleep!" Carmen cried. "What's wrong?"

Her parents didn't—or couldn't—speak. They merely held up her spy watch and pressed a button. Juni's breathless voice echoed out of the watch.

"Carmen!" he said. "Big trouble! E. Goísta is planning on kidnapping Nana. . . ."

Juni went on, telling her about E. Goísta's plan to set off the sleeping gas at midnight, during the Dos de Mayo celebration. He also warned her to guard Nana.

When Juni's speech ended, a robotic voice announced, "Message prerecorded at 11:33 P.M., May first."

Carmen glanced at the clock on her watch. What she saw made her mouth go dry.

"It's 6:34 A.M.!" she shrieked. "I fell asleep for the entire night! Where's Nana?"

Sorrowfully, Dad held out a piece of paper.

Carmen recognized her grandmother's scratchy handwriting.

Darlings, she'd written in Spanish, *Early this morning, I received a request from E. Goísta himself! He wants me to do a very special tour. He said it would last all day. I do hope you're not disappointed to attend the Dos de Mayo celebrations without me. But it is a great honor! I will see you later. In the meantime, have fun. I left a four-course meal in the icebox for you. Just nuke it when you're hungry. Love and kisses, Nana.*

"She's already gone!" Carmen squeaked. "And it's all my fault."

"Carmenita," Dad said, grabbing his daughter's shoulders. "This is not your fault! E. Goísta is wily. And he is quick. This could have happened to any spy. All that matters now is that we save the day. Not to mention, your grandmother!"

"Before midnight tonight," Mom added darkly.

"Do you think we can do it?" Dad asked Mom and Carmen.

Carmen's jaw hardened. She thought of her brother, working hard behind enemy lines. She thought of her grandmother, a sweet, unsuspecting abductee. And then she thought of those Madrileños in her dream—the ones whose lives were at stake.

"We can," Carmen declared. "We *have* to. But we need one thing if it's going to work."

"What?" Dad asked.

"We need all our family, together," Carmen admitted. "We need Juni!"

CHAPTER 11

It was some time after 6 A.M., and Juni was alone in E. Goísta's enormous kitchen. He was just putting the finishing touches on the evil architect's breakfast. In fact, he'd been so intent on preparing the meal, he'd barely slept all night. Now his eyes were red-rimmed and burning, his mouth was parched, and his hands were trembling with fatigue.

But Juni didn't care.

This meal was a masterpiece.

It was also complete, Juni realized as he delicately placed the last boiled egg in a crockery bowl. He set the timer on his spy watch for fifteen minutes. Then he surveyed the groaning spread of food.

"This will be a meal E. Goísta never forgets," he whispered to himself. "Heh, heh, heh!"

A staticky sound from his spy watch made him jump.

"Junito? Son? Are you there?"

Juni gasped and looked around. The other cooks still hadn't arrived in the kitchen—the coast was clear. Juni stole into the pantry and crouched behind a flour bin. Then he spoke into the watch.

"Dad!" he whispered. "Where has everybody been all night? I've been trying to reach you! Nana's in danger!"

"We . . . we know, Juni," Dad said. The tone in his voice said it all.

"She's . . . already gone?" Juni squeaked.

"Yes, son," Dad said, clearing his throat. "Don't worry, though. We will get her back! But first, we need *you* back! We must fight E. Goísta as a team. He's too dangerous for you to take on alone. Get out of there as soon as you can!"

"All right," Juni said, jumping to his feet. "I will. Nobody's around now, so I can make a break for it. And after all, I don't need to be here anymore. My breakfast will do my job for me. Heh-heh-heh."

"What do you mean?" Dad asked.

"Oh," Juni said. "I'll explain later. First, I've got to sneak out of here! Meet me outside the Basílica Bombardo."

"Will do," Dad said. "And, Juni—be careful!"

Juni clicked off his spy watch and returned to the kitchen. He took one last, loving glance at E. Goísta's many breakfast dishes, lined up like soldiers on the counter. Juni was sorry he wouldn't be around to see the supervillain's reaction. But Dad was right. His work here was done. It was time to leave the evil architect's headquarters.

Juni untied his butter-spattered apron and tossed it onto the butcher block. A few sleepy-eyed cooks were just stumbling into the kitchen. They gasped in surprise as they took in the array of breakfast dishes.

"Chef Radicchio," one of them said, with wide eyes. "I cannot believe my eyes. You made the entire breakfast yourself?"

"Yes," Juni said with false casualness. "I have insomnia. Cooking helps me relax. Speaking of which, I am now off to nap. I do not wish to be disturbed."

"Yes, chef," the other cooks said, bowing their heads reverentially.

Juni nodded brusquely and headed toward the living room. All he had to do now was duck back through the trapdoor in the floor and rappel down to the basilica floor. It was a good thing he had his trusty Claw 'n' Cable.

But before Juni could leave, a voice pierced the quiet bustle of the kitchen.

"Breakfast is served!"

Juni peeked over his shoulder. He saw one of E. Goísta's street-artist minions waiting, as he had the night before, at the dining room window. The cooks began passing Juni's magnificent dishes—still steaming enticingly—through the small window.

Juni nodded with determination and turned back to the living room door.

But then another voice stopped him in his tracks.

It was the voice of E. Goísta himself, wafting through the dining room window. And he was talking about . . . Juni! Or his cooking, at least.

"I cannot stop thinking about last night's incredible dinner," E. Goísta's gurgly voice was saying. "Who is the new chef?"

"It is Umberto Radicchio, Master Goísta," one of the minions answered.

"Bring him out here," E. Goísta ordered.

The minions gasped.

So did all the cooks in the kitchen.

Juni gasped so hard, he started to choke.

"But, but, master," a minion said, "you have

allowed no one to see you but us, your minions, your artists. You've always said nobody else is fit to share your presence."

"Did you *taste* those pork chops?" E. Goísta bellowed. "Clearly, the man *is* an artist. Now get him out here. I want to meet my new personal chef."

"Yes, right away, Master Goísta," said two of the minions.

"Uh-oh," Juni whispered. There was no way he could let E. Goísta meet him. He'd seen Juni's photo the day before. He'd surely recognize him as an impostor and a spy!

Juni spun around and began running through the living room. He circled the floor, searching for the trapdoor that would take him through the cathedral's false ceiling.

But he couldn't find it.

"Where'd it go?" Juni whispered desperately. He batted gold-and-silver beanbag chairs out of his way, but still, he couldn't locate the trapdoor. It blended seamlessly with the ebony floorboards. This whole cathedral was made up of optical illusions!

Juni was stuck!

What's more, two minions had just walked into

the room. One was the clown with the blue-and-red-striped face. The other was clearly a troubadour. He had a mandolin slung over his shoulder. He had long, flowing blond hair, and a hat with a big green feather in it. His nose looked like a hawk's beak.

Quickly, Juni pulled a floppy chef's hat out of his pocket and plopped it over his red curls. Then he whisked a pair of black-framed glasses off his belt. It was a lame disguise, he knew. But it was the best he could muster in the few seconds he had. What else could he do?

"You, there," the troubadour said in a lilting, beautiful tenor voice. "Radicchio?"

"What of it?" Juni said. He tried to sound haughty and arrogant, but he suspected he wasn't very convincing. His stomach was fluttering like mad.

"Boss wants to see you," the minion warbled.

"No can do," Juni shot back. "I have to run out for some . . . olive oil. It's essential to lunch. And you *know* how much E. Goísta likes his lunch."

"Someone else can get the olive oil," the troubadour said ominously. He was looking very annoyed. "When the boss wants to see you, you see the boss!"

With that, the two minions pounced on Juni, who was still so dazed by his culinary all-nighter, his fighting instincts were dulled. The minions quickly overpowered him. And before Juni knew it, they'd dragged him through the kitchen and kicked open a secret door to the dining room. They shoved him into the room.

Juni landed right before the mammoth, jiggly form of E. Goísta himself, flanked by several minions. The architect lumbered to his feet and gazed down over his enormous paunch at the Spy Kid.

"Umberto Radicchio?" the architect gurgled.

"E. Goísta?" Juni retorted.

"You are quite a chef."

"And you are quite a pig."

Juni's mouth clamped shut, but not in time to capture the insult that had just, involuntarily, escaped his lips. His hatred of this gargantuan, Nana-kidnapping, pork-chop-devouring, using-art-for-evil supervillain had gotten the better of him!

"Um, I mean," Juni stuttered, "you . . . have an admirable appetite, Master Goísta."

"Silence!" the villain roared. The nostrils of his fleshy nose flared with rage. His powder-blue pompadour quivered. And his sausagelike fingers clenched the arms of his throne-like chair.

"You dare to insult me!" E. Goísta screamed. "And after I called you a fellow artist! Clearly, I was mistaken!"

Then he swatted Juni on the head.

Juni's floppy chef's hat went flying.

His nerdy black glasses clattered to the floor.

He was exposed!

So much for the quick disguise.

E. Goísta's beady green eyes widened with recognition.

"Cortezzzzzz," he hissed. "You silly little spy. You are done for! Minions!"

Juni jumped backward and pressed himself against the dining room's florid wallpaper. Artists and musicians began to advance upon him from all sides. They clenched their fists and leered at Juni threateningly.

Juni gritted his teeth and put up his dukes. As he raised his fists in front of his face, his eyes fell upon his spy watch. The timer, which he'd entirely forgotten about in all the hubbub, was still counting down. In fact, there were only ten seconds left on it!

Suddenly, Juni relaxed. He even smiled.

Then he turned to his would-be attackers.

"Okay, guys," he said. "Before you pound me to a pulp, I have only one thing to say to you."

"*Sí?*" the troubadour sang tauntingly. "What is it?"

"Five," Juni said, "four, three, two . . . *one!*" *BOOOOOOM!*

CHAPTER 12

"**A**aaaaigh!" the minions screamed.

Boom! Boom! BOOOOOM!

One by one, the eggs that Juni had carefully stacked in the crockery bowl were exploding. Raw, slimy egg innards and sharp-edged shells pelted the villains.

"My breakfast!" E. Goísta cried as a yolk splattered on his cheek. "It's erupting!"

Juni dropped to the floor and covered his head with his hands as the eggs continued to detonate.

"You were right, E. Goísta!" he called from beneath his folded arms. "I *am* an artist. And a master chef. But I'm a spy first! And you haven't seen nothing yet."

When the last of the eggs had splattered the minions, a towering stack of blueberry pancakes began popping off the table. One hit the many-fingered guitarist square in the face. It covered his eyes and nose completely. Then it stuck fast!

"Ayeeeee!" the musician shrieked, clawing at the griddle cake frantically.

"A few supersprings and some Krazy Glue were all it took," Juni giggled to himself. Then he watched in satisfaction as the supersticky pancakes took out a couple more minions.

Next, Juni heard a huge *splooooosh!*

The Spy Kid pumped his fist happily and spun around. Sure enough, the apple cider he'd rigged with slow-acting fizz agent had just begun to spew. In a few seconds, it was spouting and splashing all over the room. A great fountain of it hit the red-and-blue-striped clown right in the face.

"Ah! Ah! Ah!" the clown cried. "I've got cider in my eyes!"

He ran screaming from the room.

In this way, every minion was conquered, one by one. They were tripped by Juni's superslick salsa. Gummed up by his murky maple syrup. Cowed by his sizzling steak and eggs.

But when the street artists had all fled the dining room, the evil architect remained. His hulking body was drenched with dripping egg yolks and plastered with gluey pancakes. Cider fizzed around the soles of his velvet slippers. An eggshell dangled off the end of his nose.

But he was still standing.

Make that, looming—right over Juni.

"You can't escape," he said. "I can squash you like a grape!"

Juni gaped up at the mammoth maniac. E. Goísta was right. Juni was no match for his hulking girth.

Not without the perfect gadget, that is.

And Juni just happened to have one tucked inside his billowing chef's pants.

It was a small, cylindrical device with a tiny whisk attached to the end of it.

"You think you can fend off the likes of *me* with a hand blender?" E. Goísta roared with a laugh. "Think again, Spy Kid."

"Oh, I have," Juni said. "This is no hand blender. It's a *Room* Blender. A little gift from my uncle Machete."

With that, Juni pushed a red button on the gizmo. Suddenly, everything in the room—the table and chairs, the trays of obliterated food remnants, even the walls—was spinning around their heads! When Juni lifted his finger from the button, he and E. Goísta had been whirled into the kitchen. A couple of chairs were teetering on top of the dry-goods shelf. Juni himself was perched on top of the pastry counter. And E. Goísta was crouched under the butcher block.

"How dare you!" the architect cried. He hauled himself to his feet and sent the butcher block flying. Then he lunged for Juni—who merely pushed the Room Blender button again!

"Aaiiiggh!" he heard E. Goísta shriek as the kitchen began to swirl once again. This time, when Juni deactivated the Room Blender, he was in the gold-and-silver living room wearing an enormous lampshade on his head. E. Goísta was perched upon a tall, metal sculpture in a corner. And the entire contents of the refrigerator were scattered over the beanbag chairs.

"Try it again, why don't you!" E. Goísta threatened. "Next time, perhaps I'll end up standing on your head."

He's got a point, Juni thought nervously. But what choice do I have?

He had to take another shot and hope the gadget would somehow blend him right out of this mess. His thumb crept toward the Room Blender's red button. He was just about to push it when he felt something give beneath his feet.

"Huh?" Juni said, looking down. Around his shoes, he saw a square of light shooting through the floorboards. And then, the square opened up entirely.

Juni had been standing directly on top of the trapdoor!

"*Aaaaah!*" he screamed as he plummeted through the small opening.

Squiiish!

That was the sound of his body passing through the basilica's false ceiling.

The next sound I hear is gonna be *splat*, Juni thought desperately. He squeezed his eyes shut and braced himself to make impact with the basilica's hard, tiled floor.

But after a few seconds, he realized all he felt was a floating sensation.

"Huh?" Juni said. He opened his eyes. He realized that the enormous lampshade, which was still on his head, had billowed out like a parachute! In another few seconds, Juni alighted gently on the church floor.

"Whew!" he breathed. He ripped the lampshade off his head and tossed it behind a pew. Then he dashed up the aisle and out into the plaza in front of the Basílica Bombardo. The courtyard was already milling with Dos de Mayo revelers. But Juni didn't see his family among them. He scanned the crowd wildly. Just when his heart had begun to sink, a strong, familiar Spanish-accented voice rang out.

"Junito!"

Juni spun around. His parents and Carmen suddenly sprang out from behind a churro stand where they'd been hiding. They bounded across the plaza to him.

"Hi!" Juni cried wildly. Before Mom or Dad had a chance to catch him up in a reunion hug, Juni threw his arms around his sister's shoulders.

"Partner!" he cried gratefully.

"Spaz!" Carmen responded, gingerly extricating herself from the unexpected hug. "What's come over you?"

Juni regained his composure and jumped backward.

"Must be battle fatigue," he said gruffly.

"Whatever," Carmen replied with equal roughness. But then, the spy sibs exchanged a secret smile. Okay, they had to admit it. They were happy to see each other.

"I hate to split us back up so soon," Mom said as she gave her disheveled son a happy squeeze, "but we've got two jobs to do. Your father and I are already on Nana's trail. So, you and Carmen have to work on the minions."

"Got it!" Juni said. "But what if we lose radio contact again? How will we find one another?"

"I thought of that already," Carmen said. She held out her hand. On it was a temporary tattoo that read OSS.

"It's a tracker," she said. "If we lose each other, the location of each tattoo will show up on our spy watches."

"Perfect," Juni said, raising his eyebrows. "Plus, it looks really cool."

Carmen handed him a square of paper. Juni licked it and slapped it onto the back of his hand. In thirty seconds, he, too, was tattooed with a black, blocky OSS.

"Excellent," he said, holding out his hand to admire the insignia.

Suddenly, Carmen's tattooed hand came down on top of his. When Juni looked up, she was staring into his eyes with determination. Juni nodded back. Then the Spy Kids looked at their parents. Mom and Dad reached over to slap their tattooed hands on top of their children's.

"Ready?" Dad cried.

"Ready!" the rest of the Cortezes shouted before breaking apart. Then Carmen turned to face her brother.

"I did a little research while you were with E. Goísta," she said. "The best place to find buskers and street artists is that place where Dad used to play soccer—the Parque del Buen Retiro."

"If we can catch them before they have a chance to leave the park, maybe we can foil E. Goísta's plan," Carmen said. "Let's just hope we get there in time."

"Well, I'm ready . . . lead the way!" Juni declared.

CHAPTER 13

As they ran through Madrid's busy streets toward the Parque del Buen Retiro, Juni recounted for Carmen everything he'd seen and heard in E. Goísta's headquarters.

Carmen slapped her hand on her forehead.

"So, basically this is all about E. Goísta's big artistic ego?" she sputtered. "Man! Makes me glad I'm a math-and-science geek!"

They trotted a few more blocks and arrived at the park entrance.

"Here we are," Carmen said, pointing at a genteel, ivy-covered arch. When the Spy Kids passed through the leafy gateway, they were transported to another world. It was quiet and breezy. Hundreds of enormous trees provided lots of soothing shade.

"This used to be a retreat for royals in the seventeenth century," Carmen informed Juni as they walked down a narrow pathway toward the park's central plaza. "Now it's still supposed to be a place of refinement. Old trees, stately fences, stone walls, and—"

"Lots of street artists," Juni added grimly. Carmen followed his gaze as they stepped onto an enormous, open plaza. She gulped.

The grounds were milling with mimes, fortune tellers, and sidewalk chalkers. Dozens of painters and a bevy of buskers were stationed around the plaza's edges.

All of the street artists seemed to be shooting one another shifty, conspiratorial glances.

"Check it out," Carmen said to Juni, pointing at one artist. "That mime has three nostrils. And look at the floppy feet on that very short sculptor."

"They've gotta be a size fifteen," Juni said grimly. "Yup, these are our guys. I'd estimate we've got at least sixty here."

"Too many to fight," Carmen said.

"And this place is too public for the Room Blender or any other serious gadgetry," Juni said as he looked around. Throngs of Madrileños were pouring steadily into the plaza. They were laughing, eating, drinking, and thoroughly enjoying the Dos de Mayo holiday. Not one of them had any idea he was in grave danger.

"This is agonizing," Juni said through gritted

teeth. "E. Goísta's minions are ripe for the picking. We just have to figure out how to pick 'em!"

Carmen didn't answer. She was staring intently at a cellist who was melodramatically sawing away at his instrument nearby. Carmen put her hand to her chin and squinted at the busker.

Then she walked over to the man. As she did, she pasted a rapturous smile onto her face. She tossed a few pesetas into the cello case at the musician's feet.

And then, Carmen began to dance.

"This is the most beautiful music I've ever heard, truly," she gushed in Spanish.

"Huh?" Juni whispered.

Suddenly, Carmen grabbed a couple of passersby by the elbows.

"Have you heard this?" she asked them. She pointed at the cellist, who by now was quite pink in the face and grinning wildly. "This man is a genius!"

Next, Carmen pointed a finger across the courtyard.

"Oh, my!" she squealed, before running over to a painter. She began exclaiming over the artist's work—a smudgy, not terribly brilliant landscape.

"It's brilliant!" Carmen pronounced loudly.

"Aw, shucks," the painter said, waving his hand with false modesty. "*Señorita*, let me paint you!"

"Do you mean it?" Carmen said loudly. Then she gazed back across the plaza at Juni and winked.

And suddenly, Juni realized what his sister was doing. She was hitting the artists right where they lived! What better way to make misunderstood artists happy than to *understand* them? Feeding their egos would starve them of their rage.

And if they no longer felt angry at the Madrileños, they'd have no reason to unleash sleeping gas upon the city!

As this realization hit Juni, he sprang into action. He began rushing from busker to musician to painter to mime, loudly praising the genius of each. Then he urged the growing numbers of Madrileños flooding the park to join in.

And before they knew it, Carmen and Juni had staged a mass art-appreciation day.

Crowds were laughing at the clowns.

Children were clamoring for the balloon sculptors' creations.

Couples were dancing to the music.

People were even quietly respecting the mimes!

All the attention made the street artists—every

last one of them—preen like peacocks. They also began performing like crazy! The musicians banded together and began playing a Mozart symphony. A troupe of actors broke into a spontaneous production of Shakespeare. The painters started sketching out a giant mural on a plaza wall.

By the time night fell, Carmen's hunch had paid off. The artists would clearly be occupied for hours.

"You think they've forgotten about E. Goísta's plan?" Juni whispered to his sister as they stole away from the joy-filled plaza.

"Completely," Carmen nodded. "Which means it's time to help Mom and Dad find Nana!"

Both Spy Kids turned their watches to their parents' frequency.

"Plan A is a lock," Carmen whispered into her watch. "How's Plan B going? Over."

The Spy Kids listened to the empty static coming out of their watches. They exchanged tense glances.

"Something's wrong," Juni whispered.

Glancing at her temporary tattoo, Carmen switched her spy watch to its tracking program. A minuscule map of Madrid popped up on the watch's screen. And flashing on that screen were two little OSS's.

"Got 'em," Carmen declared. She toggled a switch on the side of the watch and zoomed in for a closer read on her parents' locations.

"They're back at the Basílica Bombardo!" she said.

"What?" Juni whispered, feeling a chill course through him. "You mean Nana was there the entire time? I should have sensed it. I should have rescued her! And now, Mom and Dad may be in trouble, too!"

Carmen held up her hand.

"Listen," she said. "You couldn't do it all. After all, you were alone. But now's our chance. Let's go rescue Nana—*and* our parents—together."

When Carmen and Juni arrived back in the Basílica Bombardo, Juni dug into his pocket and pulled out two Huffenpuff Hot Air Pills. Bracing themselves for the awful taste, he and Carmen each popped one into their mouths. And in a few seconds, they began to float up into E. Goísta's secret headquarters.

But instead of landing in the architect's garish gold-and-silver living room, they somehow slipped through a different trapdoor. This one led to what was clearly E. Goísta's studio. The room was furnished with a few drafting tables, a wall of book-shelves, and a gold-painted desk and thronelike chair. In the center of the room was a scale model of Madrid, dotted with tiny versions of E. Goísta's garish buildings.

Not surprisingly, the decorating scheme was as ridiculous as E. Goísta himself. The vast room was dotted with pillars, each one topped by a scary stone gargoyle. A plaster mummy was propped in one corner and a dressmaker's dummy wearing a flamenco dancer's flouncy skirt stood next to it. Everywhere the Spy Kids looked, there was another over-the-top architectural detail.

But there was no Mom or Dad.

"Let's explore the rest of the apartment," Carmen said, glancing at her watch. "My tracker says they're still here."

The Spy Kids headed for the studio door. As they passed the dressmaker's dummy, Juni suddenly stopped.

"Did you hear that?" he said.

"What?" Carmen said, freezing for a moment.

"I thought I heard," Juni whispered, "sort of a high-pitched squeak. Maybe it's Mom or Nana!"

"*Eeeeeee.*"

"There it is again!" Juni cried.

Carmen shook her head.

"That sounds more like a mouse than a mom," she said. "Let's keep searching."

"You're probably right," Juni said, following Carmen to the door.

"Or then again," said a gurgly voice behind them, "maybe you're wrong!"

The Spy Kids spun around, just in time to see one of the bookshelves whoosh into the floor, disappearing entirely. And behind it, in a small, mirror-lined chamber, was a man in a voluminous satin dressing gown, bedroom slippers with wiggly horns curling off the toes, and a sinister smile.

"E. Goísta!" Juni cried.

CHAPTER 14

Juni and Carmen glared at E. Goísta.

"I should have known an evil architect like yourself would fill his headquarters with secret chambers." Juni spat.

"Yes, you should have," E. Goísta said, stepping into the studio. "But you didn't! And to think I thought the Cortezes could be a threat to me. Superspies? Ha! What a joke!"

"Take that back," Carmen said. She curled her hands into fists and dropped into her favorite kung fu launching stance. "Unless you want me to take it back for you."

E. Goísta laughed again and reached into the pocket of his dressing gown. He pulled out a fat roll of blue paper.

"Your blueprints won't help you now, E. Goísta," Juni said. "You can't build your way out of this mess!"

"Oh, no?" E. Goísta said with a snicker. Then he

gave his wrist a mighty flick. The blueprint unfurled like a whip. It stretched across the room until the end hit Carmen in the gut with a loud *snap!*

"Carmen!" Juni cried. But there was nothing he could do. The force of the stretchy blueprint's blow sent his sister flying across the room.

"Yeow!" she screamed. She crashed into the dressmaker's dummy and slumped to the floor. The dummy toppled next to her with a *splat.*

"Urgh," Carmen groaned, rubbing her stomach. Across the room, Juni glared at E. Goísta and stuck out his fists.

"Prepare for pain, Goísta!" he announced.

As Juni spoke, the whiplike blueprint snapped back into the architect's hand. He shook it threateningly at Juni.

"Or maybe *you* should!" he challenged.

"Eeeeeee."

"Wait a minute," Carmen said sharply. E. Goísta and Juni both went quiet as Carmen cocked her ear.

"Eeeeeeee. Mmmmmm."

Carmen stared at the fallen dressmaker's dummy. It sounded like that squeaking noise was coming from inside of it!

Following a hunch, Carmen brought her elbow

down on the dummy. It gave easily. In fact, it was made of wet plaster!

"Stay away from that, Cortez!" E. Goísta spat. He began to lumber across the studio toward Carmen. Juni only had to stick out his leg to trip the fleshy supervillain.

"Aaaaagh!" E. Goísta cried, tipping over like a top-heavy skyscraper. Juni jumped on the mammoth man's back, twisting his arm into a painful wrestling maneuver.

Meanwhile, Carmen was clawing away at the neck of the dressmaker's dummy. Inside, she found the paste-caked, but unmistakable, face of . . .

"Mom!" Carmen cried.

Carmen knocked the remnants of the dummy away from her mother's body. Finally, Mom was free. She spat out a mouthful of plaster and coughed painfully.

"Carmen!" she gasped.

"It's okay," Carmen said, thumping her mother on the back and stroking her matted hair.

"Your . . ." Mom choked. "Your father . . . he's in . . . the mummy."

"I'm on it!" Juni cried from across the room. He leaped off the bellowing E. Goísta and ran across the room.

"*Hi-yah!*" he yelled, giving the six-foot-tall mummy a swift kick in the middle.

The mummy—its plaster still wet—also gave way easily. In only a few seconds, Dad was free of it. Like Mom, he was coughing and choking, but okay.

"We've got . . . to find . . . your Nana!" Dad said to his children. "Who knows what horrible things E. Goísta might have done to her."

"Oh, please!" said a gurgly voice behind the family. The four spies spun around to see E. Goísta sitting in the enormous, thronelike chair behind his desk. He'd clearly regained his composure after Juni released him. His fleshy hands were folded before him and he grinned smugly.

"Your mother is just fine, Mr. Cortez," he said. "In fact, she doesn't even know she's been kidnapped. She simply thinks she's a guest in the home of the fabulous E. Goísta. I may be a supervillain, but I'm not a monster! Torturing sweet old ladies is not my style."

"Oh, well, that's a relief," Dad said. "I guess . . ."

"Torturing international superspies, however," E. Goísta said, "is another thing entirely!"

With that, he whipped a V-shaped, metal object out of his desk drawer. It was an oversized drafting compass! But where a pencil should have been, at one end of the V, there were dozens of glittering, sharp spikes instead. And E. Goísta was aiming those spikes directly at the spies' eyes!

"Oops," Juni said with a cringe. "I guess I should have tied him up before I rescued you, Dad."

"Another misstep," E. Goísta said with an evil cackle. "But this one's gonna cost you!"

E. Goísta was just pressing a trigger on his lethal drafting compass when the sound of a door slamming open made him jump. Everyone in the room gasped and turned around.

"E. Goísta!" sang a sweet, reedy voice.

"Mama!" Mom and Dad cried.

"Nana!" Juni and Carmen yelled.

"My darlings!" Nana said. She looked at her family in surprise as she walked into the studio, carrying an enormous cast-iron skillet.

"How nice to see you here!" Nana said to her family. "I was just in the kitchen, making the great E. Goísta my specialty! Paella!"

Nana thrust the skillet out toward the mad architect. His green eyes widened as he took in the sizzling golden rice and ruby-red peppers. His nostrils flared as he sniffed the plump bits of sausage and garlicky shrimp. And his fleshy lower lip quivered as he said, "That paella! It smells just like the kind my own dear Mama used to make!"

Then E. Goísta—the arrogant architect, the mad megalomaniac—burst into tears! The deadly drafting compass fell from his limp fingers and his head slumped forward.

"Oh, Mama," E. Goísta wept. "I miss her so!"

Nana patted E. Goísta's enormous back, and the evil architect began crying on her shoulder. This gave the four spies the perfect opportunity to creep up behind him. Juni snatched the drafting compass away. Carmen grabbed E. Goísta's hands and pulled them behind his back. Mom slipped a pair of handcuffs over the supervillain's wrists. And Dad deftly extricated Nana from E. Goísta's weepy embrace and led her out of the room.

"Mama," he said, taking the heavy skillet from her hand. "Come, I'll help you set the table!"

As soon as Dad had spirited Nana from the room, Mom and Carmen shoved E. Goísta into a chair and cuffed his ankles as well.

"You know how it is with Spaniards," Carmen said as she tied E. Goísta to the chair.

"Very emotional!" Juni and Mom said together. Then, while Carmen and Juni giggled, Mom planted herself in front of E. Goísta and shook her finger in his face.

"I'll *give* you something to cry about!" she scolded. "By the order of the OSS, we're placing you under arrest. Your jig is up, E. Goísta!"

Carmen and Juni turned to each other and pumped their fists.

"Yes!" they whispered.

CHAPTER 15

A few minutes later, Dad returned to E. Goísta's studio from the kitchen.

"That was a close one!" he announced. "But Mama is none the wiser—she still has no idea we are spies. She's busy now making a coconut cake for dessert."

"Thank goodness!" Mom said.

"And yum!" Juni added.

Carmen pointed to E. Goísta, who was struggling fruitlessly against his cuffs and ropes.

"And as you can see," she said to Dad, "we've handled our end of the problem as well."

That's when E. Goísta finally spoke.

"You may have me," he said. "But you don't have my minions. And they already have their orders. At midnight, on the dot, they will unleash a sleeping gas upon all of Madrid. Even you, the famous Cortezes, will not be able to contain them all! Ah-ha-ha-ha!"

"Ah-ha-ha to you!" Juni retorted. "Allow me to show you a little something, E. Goísta."

Shooting Carmen a smug wink, Juni rifled through the pockets of his baggy chef's pants. Finally, he pulled out a small brass tube.

"The good old Find & Zoom," Carmen observed with an approving nod.

The Find & Zoom was a sort of smart telescope. Type a few requests into its tiny computer, and it would seek out whatever you wanted, then zoom in for a closer look. It even had a tiny projector that would cast the image onto a wall and an audio attachment that would listen in on the scene.

"Let's see," Juni muttered. He typed "Parque del Buen Retiro" and "street artists" into the gadget. Immediately, the brass tube began to extend. Like a snake sniffing out its prey, it lengthened and slithered until its lens end poked out of E. Goísta's studio window into the night air. It began to whir and hum and pop and pivot.

And finally, an image shot out of the back end of the gadget, hitting the wall like a projected movie.

"You think you still have the support of your minions? Well, feast your eyes on this!" Carmen said to E. Goísta.

Everyone in the room watched as a troupe of actors smiled graciously and took their bows. Then, the Find & Zoom focused on the play's audience of a few hundred people, where many were clutching their hearts or wiping away tears. And they were all applauding wildly.

"But . . . but that's not right," E. Goísta sputtered.

Next, the Find & Zoom honed in on another bunch of art fans. They were lined up next to a wiry man in a dark knit cap and striped shirt. The man had a mischievous glint in his eyes and a charcoal crayon in his hand. He was drawing stacks of squares, cubes, and other angular abstractions on a large tablet.

"That's Pedro Pedresso," E. Goísta said. "A great talent, but of course, nobody understands his work. Madrileños—puh! They are not ready for his genius!"

"Oh, aren't they?" Carmen said. "Then why is there that line of people, buying Pedresso's drawings hot off the presses?"

"What?" E. Goísta gasped, squinting harder at the Find & Zoom's image. "It cannot be!"

"Oh, it is," Juni said, grinning broadly. As the Find & Zoom sought out more scenes from the plaza, however, his grin slowly faded.

"Isn't it?" he added hesitantly.

Even as he spoke, things seemed to be going sour over at the Parque del Buen Retiro.

Back at the stage, the audience was mobbing the actors for autographs. But as the fans clamored for their attention, the performers suddenly grew cold and haughty. They waved away their adoring fans.

Meanwhile, the musicians who had just finished their symphony began searching their listeners for tape recorders.

"We don't want anyone profiting from bootleg recordings!" Carmen heard her cellist friend say.

"That's gratitude for you," she muttered.

In fact, it seemed the instant the street artists began to feel appreciated, they started to take their fans' affection for granted. They grew sullen. Blasé. And worst of all, disdainful. When the Find & Zoom honed in on a balloon sculptor chatting with a mime, for instance, it caught the artists rudely turning their backs on a small crowd of adoring children.

"Sure, they like us," the sculptor said to the mime. "They don't know any better. We are casting pearls before swine."

"You're right," the mime replied. "They probably

wouldn't even *notice* if we put them to sleep. They are so worshipful and complacent!"

"Speaking of which," the sculptor muttered, "I almost forgot—there's less than hour before midnight. We've got to hit the Goístas. The boss is counting on us. Spread the word."

Then the two street artists pulled some gas masks out of their bags and began to walk out of the plaza. They motioned to other street artists as they went. The remaining artists began to exchange meaningful glances and head out of the park as well.

"I . . . I don't believe it," Juni said.

"They took their success for granted so quickly," Carmen moaned.

"That's the artistic temperament for you, kiddies!" E. Goísta cackled. "Get used to it. And while you're doing that, would you mind fetching us some gas masks? I've got some stockpiled in the closet over there."

Dad glared at the evil architect.

"Of all the puffed-up, arrogant," he said, "warped, evil—"

He would have added many more adjectives if a deep, alarmed voice hadn't interrupted him.

"Mama? Mama! Are you okay?"

The spies and the supervillain swung their heads toward the studio door again. This time, the surprise visitor was a tall man with flowing black hair and a stuffed duffel bag.

"Uncle Machete!" the Spy Kids cried. "What are you doing here?"

"Your father called and told me our mother was in trouble," Uncle Machete said. "Of course, I came immediately! Where is she? What can I do to help?"

"Perhaps you can lick the cake pans," Dad said with a smile. "She's in the kitchen making some dessert. And she's just fine, Machete."

"Oh, thank goodness," Uncle Machete said. He dropped his bag on the floor and slumped with relief into a chair. His craggy face fell into his hands. "If anything happened to Mama, I don't know what I . . . what I would . . ."

Just as tears began to spring up in Uncle Machete's eyes, Juni held up his hand.

"Wait!" he cried. He glanced at his spy watch. "Uncle Machete, you can't burst into tears yet. We've still got big trouble! And it's eleven thirty-two! We don't have a minute to lose."

"What . . . ?" Machete said.

Quickly, the other Cortezes explained the dire situation to Uncle Machete. By 11:34, he knew all about the sleeping gas and the street artists stationing themselves at every E. Goísta building in Madrid.

As they explained the situation, it began to sound even worse.

Uncle Machete blinked quizzically at the rest of his family.

"So, what's the problem?" he asked.

CHAPTER 16

"**W**hat's the problem?!" Dad sputtered. "Excuse me, big brother, but perhaps the jet lag has affected your brain? We've got twenty-six minutes before Madrid hits the hay, permanently!"

"But you've also got Carmen and Juni, the best Spy Kids in the world," Uncle Machete said confidently. "Between their wits and my gadgets, we'll get out of this fix, no problem-o."

Carmen and Juni looked at each other and gulped. But an instant later, their scared faces turned serious. Juni bent down and grabbed Uncle Machete's duffel bag off the floor.

"May I?" he asked his uncle.

"But, of course," Uncle Machete said with a nod and a sly smile.

Juni unzipped the big canvas bag and dumped its contents out onto E. Goísta's big desk. The kids began pawing through the gizmos and gadgets. Then they put their heads together and whispered.

"Hmmm," Carmen said after they separated. Then she stalked over to E. Goísta's computer and booted it up.

"What are you doing?" the architect bellowed, struggling once again to free himself from his bindings.

"It's called hacking," Carmen said calmly as she began typing briskly on the computer keyboard. "I'm just searching for a little information. Sure, I could torture it out of you, but that's not the Spy Kid style."

A few seconds later, she smiled broadly and looked over at her brother.

"Done," she said to Juni. "The sleeping gas is called Morpheus Iliac."

"That was in a top-secret, encrypted file," E. Goísta shrieked. "How did you do that?"

"Did you not hear the part about their being the best Spy Kids in the world?" Uncle Machete said to the villain. Then he, Dad, and Mom exchanged proud grins.

Meanwhile, Carmen was typing. Her fingers moved quickly over the keyboard.

"What are you doing now?" E. Goísta asked, with a desperate edge in his voice. His plump fingers were trembling, and his lips were quivering.

"Just a little Internet research into Morpheus Iliac," Carmen answered casually. Then she stopped typing.

Clearly, she'd found something.

Something big.

But her face was filled with skepticism. She was shaking her head.

"I've found a solution. But this can't be right." she said, looking up at Juni in confusion. "It's just too simple!"

"Why?" Juni said. "What counteracts Morpheus Iliac?"

Carmen shrugged and said, "Water."

"Water?" said everyone in the room.

"As in, 'Down came the rain and washed the sleeping gas out,'" Carmen said. "All we need to save the day is a thundershower."

"Well," E. Goísta cried, "I guess I win after all. It hardly ever rains in Madrid! And certainly not in May. Our rainy season just ended! It's dry as a bone out there. A thunderstorm would be absolutely impossible!"

"Did you not hear the part about my gadgets?" Uncle Machete said, pointing at the pile of gizmos on the desk. He waved his hands over the table in a grand gesture. "I have a rainmaker right here!"

"Uh, Uncle Machete?" Carmen said nervously. "Actually, he may be right. The Floodgate 2000 is really nifty. But I don't think it's nearly big enough for this job."

"No," Uncle Machete agreed. "But *these* are!"

He reached into the pile of gadgets and fished out a vial of silver pellets. Then he read the label on the container out loud: "Machete Cortez's Miracle-Flow Cloud Seeds. Simply sprinkle into a cloud, and instant rain showers ensue. Effects last for two hours."

"Okay, *fine*, you have a solution," E. Goísta sputtered. His green eyes bulged, and a vein in his temple began throbbing grotesquely. "*But* . . . you'll need a plane to get up to cloud level. And you don't have one of *those* in your little black bag, do you? Plus, you have only . . ."

E. Goísta looked wildly around the room until his eyes fell upon a cuckoo clock on the wall.

". . . eighteen minutes before midnight," E. Goísta continued. "You don't have time to find a plane. Which means, your solution is impossible." He threw back his head and laughed. "This means, I win! And you lose! Along with all of Madrid. Ah-ha-ha-ha! Now about that gas mask . . .?"

Carmen and Juni just rolled their eyes. Then

Juni reached into his pocket. He pulled out a handful of little blue balls. He gave half of them to Carmen. Then, both Spy Kids popped one of the balls into their mouths. After they grimaced their way through the melted crayon taste, they quickly floated up to the ceiling.

"Huffenpuff Hot Air Pills," Uncle Machete cried. "Of course!"

"We knew you could do it!" Mom cried proudly. She reached up to hand each of her children a small bottle of the Miracle-Flow Cloud Seeds. Then Dad passed them each a parachute and an umbrella.

"For the ride down," he noted. "*And* the rainstorm."

"Thanks!" Carmen said, strapping on the parachute and slipping the umbrella under her arm. "Now all you need to do is open the window, and we'll have the world saved in no time flat."

"Or, at least, Madrid," Juni admitted as he buckled his own parachute.

Uncle Machete threw open the big, curved windows behind E. Goísta's desk, and the Spy Kids floated up into the night air.

"Nooooooo!" they heard E. Goísta shrieking behind them.

"Oh, ignore him!" Mom called after them.

"Sorry to rain on your parade, E. Goísta!" Juni called as he sailed higher and higher.

"We'll see you soon!" Mom shouted. "When you land, we can decide what to do with the rest of our Madrid vacation!"

"And remember," Dad yelled as the Spy Kids began to disappear into a cloud. "Not a word about this to your Nanaaaaa!"

Carmen and Juni grinned and gave their parents a thumbs-up before they were swallowed up by the cloud. In a few more seconds, they'd broken through the frothy vapor. They found themselves looking down at a veritable field of clouds. It was beautiful! Carmen tore her eyes from the heavenly landscape to look at her brother, who was floating about ten feet away from her.

"Ready?" she asked.

"Ready," Juni declared. Both Spy Kids popped the cap off their bottles, then flung the shimmery silver pellets into the clouds below them.

Boooooom!

"That would be thunder!" Carmen cried.

Ssssshhhhhh. . . .

"And rain!" Juni said.

"And midnight!" Carmen added, glancing at

her spy watch. "We're just in time."

"Whoa!" Juni said, as his light, airy, buoyant feeling slowly began to seep out of his gut. "And I think our Huffenpuff Hot Air Pills have just about cooled!"

"Going dooooowwwn!" Carmen cried as she suddenly started dropping through the cloud. Juni plummeted after her. Simultaneously, the Spy Kids pulled their rip cords. Their parachutes poofed out, catching their fall and shielding them from the torrents of rain that were now coming from above them.

"Hey, look!" Carmen said, pointing to the ground, thousands of feet below. They could see clouds of green gas billowing out of every E. Goísta building in the city. But just as quickly as the gas clouds had appeared, they were visibly squelched by the onslaught of rain.

"Water!" Juni yelled, gazing happily out at the rain shower as his parachute fell gently toward the earth. "Who'd have thought it could be that easy?"

"Sort of like working together, huh?" Carmen called from her own parachute. "It definitely makes the spy work smoother."

"Absolutely," Juni said. "I'll promise never to go solo again if you will. Deal?"

Carmen gave her brother a wry grin and a thumbs-up with her OSS-tattooed hand.

"Deal! Now on to more important business," she declared. "Once we land . . ."

"Yeah?" Juni said warily.

"What," Carmen said with a grin, "are you cooking us for dinner?"